All in Reading

Book Two

by Grover K. H. Yu. Ph.D.

余光雄（Grover K. H. Yu. Ph.D.）

學歷／美國新墨西哥大學語言教育學博士
現職／南台科技大學人文社會學院院長兼
　　　應用英語系講座教授
專長／語言教育、語言測驗、媒體與傳播

三民書局

網路書店位址　http : // www.sanmin.com.tw

© All in Reading II

編著者	余光雄
發行人	劉振強
著作財產權人	三民書局股份有限公司 臺北市復興北路386號
發行所	三民書局股份有限公司 地址／臺北市復興北路386號 電話／(02)25006600 郵撥／0009998–5
印刷所	三民書局股份有限公司
門市部	復北店／臺北市復興北路386號 重南店／臺北市重慶南路一段61號

初版一刷　中華民國九十年四月
初版二刷　中華民國九十二年三月修正
初版四刷　中華民國九十五年二月
編　　號　S 803610
行政院新聞局登記證局版臺業字第○二○○號

ISBN　957–14–3286–5　（平裝）

序

　　「閱讀」在學習外（英）語的過程中佔極重要的角色。「閱讀」可說是最方便、最直接且最常用的英語學習途徑。因此，閱讀教材的好壞會直接影響到學習效果。坊間雖然有很多進口的英文教材，但由於不是針對技術學院學生及高職或綜合高中的學生編寫，以至於唸英文變成一種痛苦與折磨，教師在實際教學時也有不便之處。尤其在固定的進度壓力下，授課時數又有限，師生覺得學習英文是萬分的辛苦。

　　《全方位英文閱讀 (All in Reading)》這本英文讀本是在考慮上述諸問題的各層面，以及要幫助師生在課堂內能夠培養聽、說、讀、寫四種技能的均衡發展的需求下而編撰的。這本英文讀本的特色就是它照顧了聽、說、讀、寫四種技能的均衡發展。學生既不必為聽力訓練多帶一本課本，也不必為英文寫作多帶一本課本，因為本讀本就含有這一類的學習材料。這也就是本書取名「全方位英文」的原因。

　　筆者編撰此書時，時時刻刻想到老師要如何教，學生要如何學的問題，所以本英文讀本是以課堂教學為導向、以輕鬆有趣為方針、以生活化為原則，相信定能為學習者帶來事半功倍的效益。其中若有疏漏之處，祈請方家不吝指教。

余光雄　謹識
西元 2001 年二月
於 NKNU

All in Reading (II)
全方位英文閱讀（II）

Unit One
Stop the Spread of Deserts

 Pre-reading Activities

Recognize New Words

Learn the Chinese meaning of each bold-faced word in the following before you read the text.

1. look at a **globe**	地球；地球儀
2. the **equator**	赤道
3. this **region**	區域
4. the **desert belt**	沙漠帶

5. **crops**	農作物
6. **usable** land	可用的
7. the spread of **arid** land	乾燥的
8. to **fight back**	反抗
9. have **identified** three reasons	確認
10. the **climate pattern**	氣候型態
11. to **replace** the lost water	取代
12. **upset the balance** of nature	干擾平衡
13. a **fragile environment**	脆弱的環境
14. eat the **roots**	樹（草）根
15. leave the land **bare**	荒涼的
16. be **protected** against the dry winds	保護
17. **limit** the number of animals	限制

Brainstorming Questions

Discuss the following questions with your group members.

1. Name five biggest deserts in the world. Tell where they are. Look them up in an encyclopedia.

2. How is a desert formed?

3. How do deserts affect our living or environment?

Read the Text

Look at a globe or a map of the world. Find the deserts. Where are they? Most deserts are between 15 degrees and 30 degrees north or south of the equator. This region is the desert belt. These dry areas, such as the Sahara, the Kalahari, the

Gobi, and the Nubian, are getting larger. They are growing fast. 5
The spread of dry, useless land is a serious problem. Because
the number of people in the world is increasing, the need for food
is also becoming greater. Crops cannot grow in a desert, so
people must stop the growth of deserts. The world needs more
usable land, not less. 10

Scientists are trying to find a way to stop the spread of arid
land. They want to find ways to fight back. They are trying to
understand the reasons for desert spread.

Thus far, they have identified three reasons. The most
important reason for the spread of deserts is the climate pattern 15
of the world. Weather systems, especially the winds, over the
desert areas dry out the land. Second, there are few rivers in
these regions, so there is nothing to replace the lost water. In
addition, people have changed the land. Simple changes can
upset the balance of nature in a desert—a desert is a fragile 20
environment. However, people have needs. For example, people
need food, and they must clear land for fields and plant crops for
food. They leave the land without the natural protection of plants,
and winds can dry the land.

A third reason for the spread of deserts is the number of 25
animals. People want animals for milk and meat, but there are
too many animals for the fragile environment of these areas.
Hungry animals eat the grass, even the roots. They leave the
land bare. Then the land is not protected against the dry winds.

People cannot change the climate, but they can protect the 30
land. They can plant trees and grasses. They can limit the

number of animals too. People can be careful in their use of water and stop the spread of deserts.

Reading Comprehension Check

I: According to the text you read, put "T" in the blank if the statement is true; put "F" if it is not.

(   )   1. Most deserts are located in the areas between 15 degrees and 30 degrees north or south of the equator.

(   )   2. The Sahara desert has stopped growing since this century.

(   )   3. The world needs more usable land because the need for food is increasing.

(   )   4. The understanding of reasons of desert formation helps control the spread of deserts.

(   )   5. The climate pattern is not the major reason for the spread of deserts.

(   )   6. People cut plants which are the natural protection of land.

(   )   7. Winds do no changes to land.

(   )   8. The number of animals and human population can not be the reasons for the spread of deserts.

(   )   9. The land is left bare because people leave it without the natural protection of plants and animals eat the grass on the land.

(   )   10. No way to replace the lost water in the desert belt is one of the reasons for the spread of deserts.

II: According to the text you read, choose the best answer to each question.

(   )   1. Which of the following is the theme of the text?

(A) Paying attention to deserts in the world.

(B) Stopping the growth of deserts.

(C) Finding ways to replace the lost water on earth.

（　）2. Which of the following statements is not mentioned as one of the reasons for the spread of deserts?

(A) People clear land and leave it without any natural protection of plants.

(B) Weather systems, especially the winds, will dry out the land.

(C) There are few rivers in desert regions, so there is no way to replace the lost water.

（　）3. Why should we stop the spread of deserts?

(A) People can't grow food in a desert and the need for food is getting greater.

(B) There are fewer and fewer rivers in the world, and no way to replace water.

(C) People want animals for food and they need more land to raise animals.

（　）4. Which of the following does not account for the spread of deserts?

(A) Animals drink too much water.

(B) Animals eat the roots of plants which hold the water on in the ground.

(C) The land is left bare without any protection against the dry winds.

（　）5. According to the text, which of the following statements is not correct?

(A) Most deserts are between 15 degrees and 30 degrees north or south of the meridian.

(B) People can't change the climate, but they can protect the land.

(C) People have changed the land and upset the balance of nature in deserts.

Cloze Test I

Fill in each blank with a proper word.

Looking at a globe or a map of the world, we can find most d_____s are located between 15 degrees and 30 degrees north or south of the e_____r. This dry r_____n is called the desert belt. Believe it or not, the deserts, such as the Sahara, the Gobi, and the Nubian, are g_____y getting bigger and bigger. The spread of dry, useless land is a s_____s problem because human population in the world is i_____g, and the n_____d for food is also becoming greater. As a result, l_____d is not enough to meet the need of people. So, people must stop the g_____h of deserts. The world has to stop the s_____d of deserts.

Cloze Test II

Choose the best answer to fill in each blank to make the whole passage meaningful and grammatical.

Have you ever paid attention to the deserts in the world? Have you ever tried to look at a globe or a map to find out where the big desert _____1_____ are? If you do, you will find _____2_____ the map that these dry areas, such as the Sahara, the Gobi, the Kalahari, are mainly _____3_____ some places _____4_____ 15 degrees and 30 degrees north or south of the equator. Such _____5_____ are threatening the world because the spread of the arid, useless land is growing faster and faster. _____6_____ the number of people in the world increases, the need for food becomes greater.

(　) 1. (A) zone   (B) areas   (C) belt   (D) districts

(　) 2. (A) on   (B) between   (C) within   (D) at

(　) 3. (A) surrounded by   (B) located in
         (C) situated with   (D) protected by

(　) 4. (A) from   (B) between   (C) with   (D) of

(　) 5. (A) desserts　　　(B) deserts　　　(C) region　　　(D) zone

(　) 6. (A) According　　(B) As　　　　　(C) Because of　(D) Despite

How can we stop the spread of deserts? First of all, we must realize the reasons for desert spreading. ____7____, scientists have identified three main reasons. ____8____, the climate pattern of the world influences the weather in these regions. Weather has strong influence ____9____ our lives. Even if it is only a little change, we are affected greatly. ____10____ dry winds for example; they have strong power to dry out the land. Many ____11____ areas thus become deserts after the winds dry them out.

(　) 7. (A) Thus far　(B) Therefore　(C) However　(D) So as

(　) 8. (A) First of all　(B) In the beginning　(C) At first　(D) To begin with

(　) 9. (A) over　(B) with　(C) from　(D) of

(　) 10. (A) To take　(B) Taking　(C) Take　(D) Taken

(　) 11. (A) usable　(B) weak　(C) empty　(D) useless

Second, lacking of water is another problem. There are ____12____ rivers in these zones. ____13____, with the change in the environment, plants can not ____14____ the water on in the ground anymore. What is worse, in order to plant crops for food, people clear land and leave it ____15____ any natural protection of plants. The land ____16____. A third reason for the spread of deserts is ____17____ number of animals. By ____18____ animals in the fields, people get some milk and meat; however, animals ____19____ the fields. They eat the grass and even the roots when they are hungry. The land is becoming bare. Without plants, there is ____20____ we can do to protect the land against the dry winds.

(　) 12. (A) little　　(B) a little　　(C) few　　　(D) a few

(　) 13. (A) Besides　(B) As a result　(C) Accordingly　(D) From now on

(   ) 14. (A) hang   (B) hold   (C) keep   (D) leave

(   ) 15. (A) without   (B) giving   (C) causing   (D) reserved for

(   ) 16. (A) leave empty   (B) was left alone

           (C) is left bare   (D) leaves useable

(   ) 17. (A) a   (B) the   (C) huge   (D) increasing

(   ) 18. (A) raising   (B) arising   (C) rising   (D) feed

(   ) 19. (A) tremble   (B) trample   (C) temple   (D) temper

(   ) 20. (A) nothing   (B) something   (C) anything   (D) everything

        __21__ , to prevent the deserts from growing, we can plant plants, such as trees and grasses as many as possible. Also, we can limit the number of animals that are raised for food. Although natural power is __22__ strong that we can't change the climate, we can protect our environment from __23__ . __24__ , we must think what may happen to us if the earth is not suitable for us to live on. We must consider the future of our next generations. If we don't protect natural resources of the great Nature, what our future generations can __25__ ?

(   ) 21. (A) To tell the truth   (B) In addition   (C) As a result   (D) To sum up

(   ) 22. (A) too   (B) so   (C) quite   (D) extremely

(   ) 23. (A) destroying   (B) destroy

           (C) being destroying   (D) being destroyed

(   ) 24. (A) After all   (B) Meanwhile   (C) In conclusion   (D) Later on

(   ) 25. (A) eat with   (B) do with it   (C) survive from   (D) live on

Developing Linguistic Ability

Word Definition

Match each of the words in the left column with its definition given in the right column.

_____ 1. globe   (A) agricultural products

_____ 2. spread (*n.*)   (B) dried land

_____ 3. desert   (C) stretch; extent of space

_____ 4. region   (D) the earth

_____ 5. crop   (E) area, zone

_____ 6. belt   (F) to recognize or discover

_____ 7. increase   (G) dry; having no rain

_____ 8. arid   (H) the typical weather conditions in a particular area

_____ 9. identify   (I) a large area of land with particular characteristics

_____10. climate   (J) to get bigger in number; to add

_____11. replace   (K) empty; no covering

_____12. balance   (L) to keep in a state of equality

_____13. fragile   (M) to take the place of; to substitute

_____14. environment   (N) easily broken or damaged

_____15. bare   (O) surroundings

Vocabulary in Use

Choose the correct answers.

(   ) 1. _____ land is so dry that very few plants can grow on it.

      (A) Usable   (B) Arid   (C) Swamp   (D) Bare

(   ) 2. If health _____ with wealth, that means both things are of equal importance.

    (A) replaces   (B) balances   (C) surrounds   (D) decays

(   ) 3. A(n) _____ is a strip of leather that one can use to fasten around his or her waist.

    (A) stripe   (B) zone   (C) area   (D) belt

(   ) 4. If a part of the body is _____, it means it is not covered by anything.

    (A) bare   (B) fragile   (C) injured   (D) exposed

(   ) 5. The general weather conditions that are typical of a certain place is the _____ of that place.

    (A) temperature   (B) surrounding   (C) climate   (D) custom

(   ) 6. _____ are plants such as wheat and vegetables that we grow for food.

    (A) Crops   (B) Flops   (C) Drops   (D) Props

(   ) 7. A(n) _____ is a large area where there is almost no water, no plants at all.

    (A) dessert   (B) island   (C) swamp   (D) desert

(   ) 8. Glass is very _____ because it can be broken easily.

    (A) expensive   (B) fragile   (C) fragrant   (D) elegant

(   ) 9. We can refer to the world as the _____ when we emphasize how big it is.

    (A) globe   (B) glove   (C) glow   (D) growth

(   ) 10. When something becomes bigger in number, we say it is _____.

    (A) increasing   (B) fragile   (C) spreading   (D) arid

Idiom and Phrase

Match each of the following phrases in the left column with its Chinese definition given in the right column.

_____ 1. find ways to solve   (A) …的理由

_____ 2. thus far   (B) 除…之外

_____ 3. dry out   (C) 設法解決

_____ 4. in addition   (D) 另外；還有

_____ 5. in the north of...   (E) 對…之需要

_____ 6. in addition to...   (F) 使乾燥

_____ 7. reason for   (G) 在…要小心

_____ 8. protect...against...   (H) 在…之北

_____ 9. be careful in...   (I) 到目前為止

_____ 10. the need for...   (J) 保護…免受…

Phrase in Use

Fill in each blank with a proper phrase from the box. Make some changes, if necessary.

thus far	reason for	find ways to	dry out	protected against
north of	in addition	careful in	need for	in addition to

1. Taiwan has a strong _____ a high speed railway.

2. The water in the lake has to be well _____ pollution.

3. There are too many _____ us to learn to use computers.

4. _____ providing nutrition, this food really tastes very delicious.

5. No city officers have _____ solve traffic problem.

6. _____, I've told you all I knew. I've got nothing to tell.

7. Clothes _____ very fast in dry climate.

8. _____, health and wealth are like both hands of one's body.

9. Tainan is located in the _____ Kaohsiung city.

10. For happiness, you must be _____ choosing your lifelong partner.

Vocabulary Development

Synonyms: Give one proper synonym to each of the following words.

1. globe → _____   4. desert → _____

2. identify → _____   5. careful → _____

3. region → _____   6. environment → _____

Antonyms: Give one antonym to each of the following words.

1. increase → _____   4. fragile → _____

2. usable → _____   5. arid → _____

3. balance → _____   6. spread (*v.*) → _____

Grammar Focus

> Rule 1: The phrases '**so far**,' '**thus far**' and the connective '**since**' are often used in the present perfect tense.

Examples:

1. **Thus far**, scientists **have identified** three reasons for the spread of deserts.

2. **So far**, I**'ve learned** English for at least six years.

3. I **have not seen** Tony for years **since** he moved to Taipei.

> Rule 2: The verbs such as '**get, become, grow, seem, look, feel, smell**' can be followed by adjectives which function as subjective complement.

Examples:

1. We are getting **older** as days go by.

2. In winter, days become **shorter**.

3. After the long journey, all of us <u>felt</u> **tired**.

4. Roses <u>smell</u> **sweet**.

5. Boys usually <u>grow</u> **taller** than girls.

6. They <u>seemed</u> **unhappy** when they arrived.

Grammar Exercise

Use your own words to complete the following sentences.

1. The argument seems to be _____. （冗長）

2. As we grow _____, we become _____ and _____.

3. After being sick for a while, she felt very _____. （虛弱）

4. With the given evidence, the murder case becomes _____. （明顯）

5. The food smells _____.

6. The rich people get _____ and the poor get _____. That's
   bad.

Sentence-pattern Focus

◎*Sentence Pattern I*

A. Affirmative: A＋Be-verb＋**as**＋原級形容詞＋**as**＋B

B. Negative: A＋Be-verb＋**not so** (or **as**)＋原級形容詞＋**as**＋B

Examples:

1. He is **as strong as** his brother.

2. He is **not so strong as** his brother.

◎*Sentence Pattern II*

A. A＋Be-verb＋比較級形容詞＋**than**＋B

B. A＋Be-verb＋**the**＋比較級形容詞＋**of the two**

C. A＋Be-verb＋**less**＋原級形容詞＋**than**＋B

Examples:

1. He is **older than** she.

2. He is **the older of the two**.

3. She is **less active than** he.

　→ She is **not as active as** he.

　→ He is **more active than** she.

◎*Sentence Pattern III*

A. Affirmative:

　A＋Be-verb＋**the**＋最高級形容詞＋**of** (or **among**)＋**the three** (or **all**)

B. Negative:

　A＋Be-verb＋**the least**＋原級形容詞＋**of** (or **among**)＋**the three** (or **all**)

Examples:

1. Helen is **the most impatient of the three**.

2. Helen is **the least impatient of the three**.

Structure in Use

Translate each of the following Chinese sentences into English.

1. 到目前為止沒有人能長生不老。

　_____

2. 自從畢業後，我們還沒得到她的消息。

　_____

3. Betty 是兩者中較為堅強的。

　_____

4. Tony 沒有我跑得快。

　_____

5. 五人之中 James 最不挑剔 (picky)。

_____

Sentence Combination

Use the given hints to make your own sentences.

1. [Hint] James is strong. Peter is strong, too.

   → James _____.

2. [Hint] Betty is smart. Grace is smarter.

   → Grace is _____.

   → Betty is _____.

3. [Hint] Peter has $500 dollars. Sam has $700 dollars. Bob has $1,000 dollars.

   → Bob is _____.

   → Peter is _____.

   → Sam is _____.

4. [Hint] In winter, the temperature in Taipei is 18 degrees Celsius. In Taichung, it is 20 degrees Celsius. In Kaohsiung, it is 22 degrees Celsius most of the time.

   → In winter, Kaohsiung is _____ than _____.

   → In winter, Taipei is _____ of the three cities.

   → Taichung is neither _____ than _____, nor _____ than _____.

5. [Hint] Gold is valuable. Diamond is more valuable.

   → Diamond is _____ of the two.

   → Gold is _____ than _____.

Derivations of Words: Morphology

Fill in each of the following blanks with the appropriate form of the word given.

1. They are very _____ (science) in their approach.

2. Can I see your _____ (identify) card, please?

3. The _____ (globe) climate has changed a lot recently.

4. Language may have _____ (region) differences in pronunciation.

5. Are used plastic materials still _____ (use)?

 Speaking Activities

Group Discussion

Discuss the following questions with your group members. Then, report your answers to the class.

1. How do we know that the deserts are spreading?

2. What are the possible causes of desert spread?

3. What can people do to stop the spread of deserts?

Dialogue Completion

Complete the following dialogue.

A: Where can we see deserts on earth?

B: Most of them are located _____ of the equator.

A: What do we call these areas?

B: They are called _____.

A: Do you know the biggest desert in China?

B: The _____.

A: How big is it?

B: It is _____.

A: Why do we need to protect forests?

B: Forests can help _____.

A: What may happen if people leave the land without any natural protection and let the winds dry it out?

B: _____

A: Why is it difficult to grow plants on deserts?

B: _____

Listening Activities

Sentence Dictation

Listen to the tape, and then fill in the following blanks with the missing words.

1. Scientists want to _____ back against the spread of _____ land.

2. _____ cannot grow in deserts, so we must stop the _____ of deserts.

3. There is nothing to _____ the lost water on the land.

4. The land is left _____, not well _____ against the winds.

5. There are too many animals for the _____ _____.

6. People cannot change the _____, but they can _____ the land.

7. People can be careful _____ their use of water so as to help stop the desert _____.

8. Animals _____ the land without the natural _____ of plants.

9. Simple changes can _____ the _____ of nature in a desert.

10. _____ have found a way to _____ the spread of arid land.

Listen and Answer

Listen to the narrations and questions on tape. Then answer the questions by completing the following sentences.

1. Scientists are trying to _____.

2. They are located between _____.

3. _____ reasons for the spread of deserts have been identified by scientists .

4. They can _____.

5. These changes can _____.

Dialogue Comprehension

Listen to the dialogues on tape, and then answer the questions by completing the following sentences.

1. They are talking about _____.

2. The reason is _____.

3. The whole globe is _____.

4. He is concerned about _____.

5. She suggested that we can _____, and try not to
_____.

Writing Activities

Translation

Translate the following chinese sentences into English.

1. 沙漠擴大主要是因為全球氣候型態的緣故。

   The main reason for _____.

2. 單純的變化能擾亂沙漠中的自然平衡。

   Simple changes _____.

3. 人們不能改變氣候，但可以保護土地。

   People cannot _____.

4. 人們可以種植樹或草來防止水的流失。

People can grow _____.

5. 人口的控制及土地保護可以防止沙漠的擴大。

Population control _____.

6. 隨著時光消逝，我們變老了。

We are getting _____ _____ days go by.

7. 在冬天，白天變短了。

In winter, _____ become _____.

8. 玫瑰散發香味。

Roses smell _____.

9. 男孩通常長得比女孩高。

Boys usually _____ _____ than girls.

10. 當他們到達時，他們似乎不快樂。

They _____ _____ when they arrived.

Sentence Completion

Use your own words to complete the following sentences.

1. There are few _____, so there is nothing to _____.

2. A good reason for _____ is _____.

3. A main reason for _____ is that _____.

4. People cannot _____, but they can _____.

5. We can be careful in _____.

Unit Two

Welcome to the Web

 Pre-reading Activities

Recognize New Words

Learn the Chinese definition of each bold-faced word in the following before you read the text.

1. see **scenes**	場景
2. from the **latest** movies	最新的
3. get free **versions**	版本
4. **brand-new** computer programs	全新的

5. **characters**   人物；角色

6. **the latest cartoons**   最新卡通

7. **samples** of songs   樣本

8. **browse** through museums   瀏覽

9. **statues of dinosaurs**   恐龍塑像

10. the **space shuttle**   太空梭

11. **photographs** of TV stars   照片

12. a **giant** book   巨大的

13. **animated cartoons**   卡通動畫

14. the **Internet**   網際網路

15. **a bunch of wires**   一束電線

16. **cables** connecting computers   電纜

17. **allows** people **to**...   允許…

18. to **exchange** exciting information   交換

19. quickly and **inexpensively**   便宜地

20. **hooking** your computer to...   連結

21. lines **attached to** your house   連結

22. the **local** library   地方的；當地的

23. **connect** to the Internet   連結

Brainstorming Questions

Discuss the following questions with your group members.

1. What does WWW stand for?

2. Do you know how to get access to the World Wide Web?

3. What are the advantages of surfing the Internet?

Read the Text

Would you like to go to a place where you can see scenes from the latest movies, play games with people from all around the world, and get free versions of brand-new computer programs?

If you go to this place, you might meet characters from the latest cartoons, hear samples of songs that haven't even come out yet, or learn the news before it appears on TV. Or, if you prefer, you can browse through museums, admiring beautiful paintings or statues of dinosaurs. You can look out the window of the space shuttle, listen to radio stations on the other side of the country, and even collect photographs of your favorite TV stars.

What is this place? It's called the World Wide Web. Like a giant book, the Web is full of pictures and words, but you'll find a lot of things you've never seen in a book before, such as animated cartoons and computer programs. And you get there, believe it or not, through a computer.

The World Wide Web is part of the international computer network called the Internet. What is the Internet? In a sense, it's just a bunch of wires and cables connecting millions of computers around the world. That may not sound very exciting in itself, but the Internet allows people all over the world to exchange exciting information quickly and inexpensively. By hooking your own computer to this network of wires through the telephone lines attached to your house, or by using special computers at your school or the local library, you can connect right to the

5

10

15

20

25

Internet yourself.

And then you can be a part of the World Wide Web!

Reading Comprehension Check

I: According to the text you read, if the statement is true, put "T" in the blank; if not, put "F" in the blank.

(　　) 1. We can't browse through museums on the Internet.

(　　) 2. People can listen to radio stations on the other side of the country through the Internet.

(　　) 3. The World Wide Web is full of pictures and words.

(　　) 4. The World Wide Web is part of the international computer network called the Internet.

(　　) 5. The Internet allows people all over the world to exchange exciting information quickly and inexpensively.

II: According to the text you read, complete the following sentences.

1. You can connect to the Internet by _____ to the network of wires through _____ lines attached to _____
   _____.

2. The Internet is just a bunch of _____ connecting _____
   _____ around the world.

3. The Internet enables us to get _____ versions of _____
   _____ programs.

4. The World Wide Web is part of _____
   called the Internet.

5. The Internet allows people to _____ quickly and inexpensively.

Developing Linguistic Ability

Vocabulary Development

Synonyms: Give one synonym to each of the following words.

1. connect → _____   4. inexpensive → _____

2. arid → _____   5. giant → _____

3. allow → _____

Antonyms: Give one antonym to each of the following words.

1. inexpensive → _____   4. exciting → _____

2. brand-new → _____   5. quickly → _____

3. giant → _____   6. part → _____

Morphology

I. The prefix 'in-,' 'im-,' 'un-' or 'dis-' means 'no/not.' Add one of them to each of the following words to form a different word.

1. expensive → _____   6. connect → _____

2. appear → _____   7. happy → _____

3. believable → _____   8. believe → _____

4. hook → _____   9. partial → _____

5. locate → _____   10. polite → _____

II. Add the suffix '-tion' to each of the following verbs to form the noun.

1. animate → _____   5. connect → _____

2. admire → _____   6. collect → _____

3. educate → _____   7. communicate → _____

4. sense → _____

Word Definition

Match each of the words in the left column with its definition given in the right column.

_____ 1. version   (A) a new form of an original model

_____ 2. local   (B) a set of wires

_____ 3. a bunch   (C) to inspect in a casual way

_____ 4. brand   (D) of a certain place

_____ 5. allow   (E) a group or a cluster

_____ 6. connect   (F) to link

_____ 7. cable   (G) to let happen

_____ 8. exchange   (H) a trademark

_____ 9. browse   (I) to give and receive something in return for something else

_____10. sample   (J) a small part representing th whole

Vocabulary in Use

Copy the best answer to fill in the blank in each sentence.

(　　) 1. You can _____ your personal computer to the Internet through the telephone lines.

    (A) exchange   (B) hook   (C) allow   (D) add

(　　) 2. Children's favorite TV programs are _____.

    (A) soap operas   (B) weather reports   (C) cartoons (D) news

(　　) 3. Mom doesn't _____ me to watch TV unless I finish my homework.

    (A) ask   (B) allow   (C) agree   (D) approve

(   )   4. It's a custom to _____ presents on the Christmas party.

      (A) exchange   (B) send   (C) purchase   (D) choose

(   )   5. _____ news lets us know what's happening around our surround-ings.

      (A) Urban   (B) Local   (C) Suburban   (D) Rural

(   )   6. Father gets the habit of _____ several copies of newspapers every day.

      (A) previewing   (B) reviewing   (C) borrowing   (D) browsing

(   )   7. After _____ to the Internet, I had an adventure in a brand new world.

      (A) allowing   (B) believing   (C) connecting   (D) exchanging

(   )   8. I enjoyed the _____ in Canada when I went traveling last summer. It's very peaceful and magnificent.

      (A) scene   (B) view   (C) web   (D) version

(   )   9. The bus line _____ the two citys.

      (A) catches   (B) attaches   (C) connects   (D) repeats

(   ) 10. Through the Internet, fans of Tom Cruise can easily collect many _____ of his.

      (A) photographs (B) telegrams   (C) cell phones   (D) spectrograms

Phrase in Use

Choose the correct answers.

(   )   1. If you don't have enough time to read your book carefully, you may try to _____ it.

      (A) attach to   (B) connect to   (C) hook up to   (D) browse through

(   ) 2. Children enjoy reading story books _____ abundant pictures.

      (A) full of   (B) afraid of   (C) in case of   (D) because of

( ) 3. By _____ your computer _____ the network of wires through telephone lines, you can connect to the Internet.

(A) changing...to (B) setting...apart

(C) hooking...to (D) allowing...to

( ) 4. _____, computers are just machines that we use. They can't do everything for us.

(A) In a word (B) In a sense (C) In reality (D) In case

( ) 5. I've lost _____ keys in the classroom yesterday. Have anyone found it?

(A) a piece of (B) a group of (C) a part of (D) a bunch of

Structure Focus

Follow the sentence structures given below to create your own sentences.

1. If you go to this place, you might meet characters from the latest cartoons.

a. If you visit a museum, you might _____.

b. If you _____, you might _____.

2. By hooking your own computer to the network of wires, you can get access to the Internet.

a. By traveling around the world, you _____.

b. By _____, _____.

3. Would you like to go to a place where you can see the latest movies?

a. Would you like to eat dinner with _____?

b. Would you like to _____?

4. The World Wide Web is part of the international computer network.

a. _____ is part of _____.

b. _____ is part of _____.

5. Like a giant book, the Web is full of pictures and words.

a. Like a superman, _____.

b. Like Mozart, _____.

 Speaking Activities

Dialogue Practice

Find a partner to practice the following dialogue.

Situation: A and B meet in the student union.

A: I have found a fun place for entertainment.

B: Where is it? What do you do there?

A: I'll tell you where it is. At this place I can see the latest movies, and play free games.

B: That sounds like a great place.

A: Not only that. I can also meet cartoon characters, hear popular songs, learn some news, and browse through museums to admire beautiful paintings.

B: How much do you have to pay for all of these? It seems quite an interesting place, isn't it?

A: Yah, you bet! It is called the World Wide Web.

B: What's the World Wide Web?

A: It's an international computer network called the Internet, which connects millions of computers around the world with wires and cables.

B: How can I get on the World Wide Web?

A: It's easy. You just need to hook your own computer to this network of wires through telephone lines.

B: Is that all? That's really simple and easy. How much does it cost?

A: It costs the same as your telephone service charges.

 *Listening Activities*

Sentence Comprehension

If the sentence you hear on tape means the same as the one you read the below, put "S" in the blank; if not, put "D" in the blank.

_____ 1. You can get free versions of brand-new computer programs.

_____ 2. You can connect your own computer to the Internet by yourself.

_____ 3. The Internet allows people all over the world to exchange information.

_____ 4. You can listen to the radio stations on the other side of the country.

_____ 5. By using special computers, you can connect to the Internet.

_____ 6. You can be a part of the World Wide Web.

Sentence Dictation

Listen to the tape, and then fill in the blanks with the missing words.

1. The World Wide Web is the international computer _____ which is just a bunch of wires and _____ connecting millions of computers around the world.

2. The World Wide Web, like a _____ book, is full of pictures and words.

3. The Internet may not sound very exciting in itself, but it allows people all over the world to _____ exciting information quickly and _____.

4. By _____ your own computer to this network of wires through the telephone lines _____ to your house, you can connect right to the Internet yourself.

5. You can see _____ from the latest movies, play games with people from all around the world, and get free _____ of brand-new computer programs on the World Wide Web.

Sentence Memory

Listen to the sentences on tape carefully. If the two sentences you hear mean the same, put "S" in the blank; if not, put "D" in the blank.

1. _____ 2. _____ 3. _____ 4. _____ 5. _____

Listen and Answer

Listen to the narrations and questions on tape. Then answer the questions by completing the following sentences.

1. I can get _____ from _____.

2. The Internet is just _____ connecting _____.

3. I can connect to the Internet by _____
   through _____.

4. The World Wide Web is like _____.

5. I can see scenes from the latest movies, and play games with people from all
   around the world on _____.

Dialogue Comprehension

Listen to the dialogues on tape, and then answer the questions by completing the following sentences.

1. She can get to the World Wide Web by _____.

2. People can play games with others from all over the world _____.

3. We can find _____.

4. They collect them _____.

Writing Activities

Sentence Completion

Use your own words to complete the following sentences.

1. You can look out the window of _____.

2. Like a giant book, the Web is full of _____.

3. The World Wide Web is part of _____.

4. The Internet allows people to _____.

5. By using computers at your school, you can _____.

Sentence Scrambling

Re-arrange the given chunks of words to form grammatical sentences.

1. of brand-new computer programs/will help you/the World Wide Web/get free versions

   → _____

2. the latest cartoons/from/characters/meet/might/you

   → _____

3. the space shuttle/look out/can/the window/we/of

   → _____

4. before/never/seen/you've/in a book/animated cartoons

   → _____

5. computers/in our lives/believe it or not/one of the important tools/have become

   → _____

Translation

Translate the following Chinese sentences into English.

1. 你可以從網際網路上收集你喜歡的電視明星照片。

   You can _____ _____ of your _____ TV stars on the _____ .

2. 如果你喜歡，你可以瀏覽博物館，欣賞美麗的畫作或恐龍塑像。

   If you _____ , you can _____ _____ museums, _____ beautiful paintings or _____ of dinosaurs.

3. 全球資訊網是國際電腦網路——網際網路的一部分。

   The _____ _____ _____ is part of the _____ _____ _____ called the _____ .

4. 你可以從太空梭的窗子向外看。

   You can _____ _____ the window of the _____ _____ .

5. 就像一本巨大的書一樣，網站充滿各式各樣的圖片和文字。

   _____ a giant book, the Web is _____ _____ various kinds of pictures and words.

Error Correction

In the following passage, some underlined parts are grammatically incorrect and some are not. Correct the errors, or put a "○" in the blank if the underlined part is correct.

The World Wide Web (1) are part of the international computer network called the Internet. What is (2) Internet? In a sense, it's just (3) a bunch of wire and cables (4) to connect millions of computers around the world. That may not sound very (5) excited in itself, but the Internet allows people all over the world (6) exchanging exciting (7) informations quickly and inexpensively. (8) From hooking your own computer (9) with this network of wires through the telephone lines (10) <u>attaching</u> to your house, or by using (11) <u>the special computers</u> at your school or the local library, you can connect right (12) <u>from</u> the Internet yourself.

Answers:

(1) _____   (2) _____   (3) _____

(4) _____   (5) _____   (6) _____

(7) _____   (8) _____   (9) _____

(10) _____   (11) _____   (12) _____

Unit Three
Communication through Satellite

 Pre-reading Activities

Learn the Chinese definition of each bold-faced word in the following before you read the text.

1. communications **satellites**	衛星
2. **rockets**	火箭
3. **kilometers**	公里
4. Earth's **surface**	表面

5. in a great **circle**	圓圈
6. an **orbit**	軌道
7. around our **planet**	行星
8. **signals**	信號
9. **relay** the signals	傳遞
10. **rapid**	快速的
11. a **reflection** of	反射
12. **bounce off**	反彈
13. **devices**	設計；設備
14. **amplify or strengthen** them	擴張或強化
15. **the Atlantic Ocean**	大西洋
16. **at one time**	一次；一下子
17. **microwaves**	微波
18. travel **in straight lines**	以直線方式
19. **transmit** the signal	傳遞
20. **technicians**	技術人員
21. **at an angle**	以某種角度
22. **one third of...**	三分之一的…
23. **instantaneous**	立即的
24. an **event**	事件

Read the Text

High above the Earth, there are communications satellites. Rockets take them high into the sky, usually about 22,300 miles, or 35,900 kilometers, above the Earth's surface. Like the moon, Earth's only natural satellite, communications satellites travel in a

great circle (an orbit) around our planet. Most of these satellites   5
travel at the same speed as the Earth, so they seem to be
always in the same place in the sky. Stations on the ground,
called Earth stations, send signals to these satellites. They carry
equipment to relay (send on) the signals. Because of these
satellites, communication can be easy and rapid.   10

The first communications satellites were like sound or signal
mirrors. Like a person looking in a mirror, the returning signal
was a reflection of the first signal. Messages bounced off the
satellite like a ball on a road. Today, however, communications
satellites are all active devices. They receive the signals, amplify   15
or strengthen them, and then relay them. The communications
satellites over the Atlantic Ocean can carry more than 30,000
telephone calls at one time.

As these satellites circle the Earth, messages are sent to
them with radio waves (microwaves). Waves like radio signals   20
travel in straight lines. By using a satellite to receive and then
transmit the signal (that is, relay the message), technicians are
sure that the messages will continue. The waves travel in a
straight line up (at an angle) to a satellite and then in a straight
line down to the Earth at an angle. Because there are a large   25
number of these communications satellites, a message can go
up and down as many times as necessary to reach anyone
anyplace on the planet. One satellite at 22,300 miles above the
Earth can send signals to about one third of the planet.
Therefore, with three satellites in the proper places, messages   30
can go everywhere on Earth. Satellite communication happens

so fast that it is almost instantaneous.

These satellites make it possible for an event in one part of the world to be seen on television everywhere. Telephone calls between any two places on Earth are now possible.   35

Reading Comprehension Check

I: According to the text you read, if the statement is true, put "T" in the blank; if not, put 'F' in the blank.

(   ) 1. Airplanes take communications satellites high into the sky.

(   ) 2. Most of these satellites around our planet seem to be always in the same place in the sky.

(   ) 3. Today communications satellites were like sound or signal mirrors.

(   ) 4. One satellite can send signals to about two thirds of the Earth.

(   ) 5. Because of the satellites, communication between any two places on Earth are now possible.

II: According to the text you read, complete the following sentences.

1. Like the _____, satellites travel in a great _____ around the Earth.

2. As these satellites circle the Earth, messages are _____ to them with radio _____.

3. Waves like _____ signals travel in _____ lines.

4. With _____ satellites in the proper places, messages can go _____ on Earth.

5. _____ _____ between any two places on _____ are now possible.

III: According to the text you read, select the best answer to each of the following questions.

(　　) 1. With what are messages sent to the Earth?

      (A) Rockets.　(B) Radio waves.　(C) Sound.　(D) Signal mirrors.

(　　) 2. How many times can a message go up and down to the Earth?

      (A) As many times as necessary.　(B) Three times.

      (C) Twice.　(D) Once.

(　　) 3. How many telephone calls can the satellites over the Atlantic Ocean carry at one time?

      (A) 22,300.　(B) 21,000.　(C) 35,900.　(D) 30,000.

(　　) 4. One satellite at 22,300 miles above the Earth can send signals to about

      _____.

      (A) two fourths of the Earth　(B) two thirds of the Earth

      (C) one third of the Earth　(D) one fourth of the Earth

(　　) 5. How many satellites do we need at least to make messages go everywhere on Earth?

      (A) Four.　(B) Three.　(C) Five.　(D) Six.

Developing Linguistic Ability

Vocabulary Development

Synonyms: Give one synonym to each of the following words.

1. large → _____   4. anyplace → _____

2. rapid → _____   5. anybody → _____

3. relay → _____   6. however → _____

Antonyms: Give one antonym to each of the following words.

1. rapid → _____   4. high → _____

2. everywhere → _____   5. above → _____

3. great → _____   6. strengthen → _____

Morphology

I: The prefix 'in-,' 'im-' or 'un-' means 'no/not.' Choose one of them to add to each of the following words to form a different word.

1. expensive → _____   4. easy → _____

2. natural → _____   5. proper → _____

3. possible → _____   6. necessary → _____

II: Add the suffix '-tion,' '-ity' or '-ness' to each of the following words to form the noun.

1. animate → _____   4. possible → _____

2. rapid → _____   5. large → _____

3. active → _____   6. reflect → _____

Parts of Speech

Give the proper form of the following words.

Noun	Verb	Adjective
1. _____	_____	active
2. _____	reflect	_____
3. communication	_____	_____
4. _____		rapid
5. _____	strengthen	_____

Word Definition

Match each of the words in the left column with its definition given in the right column.

_____ 1. communication

_____ 2. satellite

_____ 3. surface

_____ 4. circle

_____ 5. device

_____ 6. planet

_____ 7. instantaneous

_____ 8. amplify

_____ 9. relay

_____ 10. signal

(A) a large body in space that moves around a star

(B) to pass or send along from one group or station to another

(C) happening at once

(D) the exchange of thoughts, messages, or information

(E) to make larger or more powerful

(F) the outer part

(G) a man-made object which moves around a planet

(H) a sign, device, or other indicator serving as a means of communication

(I) an instrument, especially one that is cleverly thought out

(J) a curved line that is everywhere equally distant from one fixed point

Vocabulary in Use

Choose the correct answers.

(　　) 1. As satellites circle the Earth, _____ are sent to them with radio waves.

(A) light　(B) pictures　(C) voices　(D) messages

(　　) 2. People in Taiwan today _____ abroad more often than before.

(A) walk　(B) travel　(C) ride　(D) invite

(   )   3. She has _____, not curly hair.

       (A) long   (B) round   (C) square   (D) straight

(   )   4. It's _____ to make a monkey do things like a mankind.

       (A) possible   (B) normal   (C) unusual   (D) different

(   )   5. He says that he wants to visit every city _____ the island.

       (A) between   (B) above   (C) about   (D) on

(   )   6. The beautiful girl looked herself in a _____.

       (A) mirror   (B) planet   (C) rocket   (D) satellite

(   )   7. The basketball game was _____ live in America and Taiwan.

       (A) circled   (B) bounced   (C) strengthened   (D) transmitted

(   )   8. Jogging can _____ the functions of the heart and lungs.

       (A) large   (B) strengthen   (C) power   (D) reduce

(   )   9. It's easy to _____ the boxes into the room.

       (A) fix   (B) catch   (C) carry   (D) use

(   ) 10. The ball _____ off the pitcher's glove. He didn't catch the ball.

       (A) relayed   (B) amplified   (C) bounced   (D) got

Phrase in Use

Choose the correct answers.

(   ) 1. It is _____ hot _____ we'd better stay in the air-conditioned

      house.

       (A) too...to   (B) both...and   (C) so...so   (D) so...that

(   ) 2. There are _____ mosquitos in the park, so I don't like to take a walk

      there.

       (A) a large number of   (B) a volume of   (C) a little   (D) the box of

(   ) 3. Can you watch TV and talk on the telephone _____?

       (A) right now   (B) at one time   (C) at all times   (D) at that moment

( ) 4. He says that he can run at _____ speed _____ Johnson.

    (A) more...than   (B) as...as   (C) the same...as   (D) so...as

( ) 5. There are _____ one million people in Kaohsiung.

    (A) less than   (B) fewer than   (C) better than   (D) more than

( ) 6. We _____ we will succeed some day if we work hard every day.

    (A) are sorry that   (B) are sure of

    (C) are sure that   (D) are sure to

( ) 7. The man bounced the child _____ on his knees.

    (A) off and on   (B) off and up   (C) off and down   (D) up and down

Structure Focus

Follow the sentence structures given below to create your own sentences.

1. Because of these satellites, communication can be easy and rapid.

    a. Because of the modern conveniences, life _____.

    b. Because of _____.

2. Satellite communication happens so fast that it is almost instantaneous.

    a. The air crash happened so fast that _____.

    b. _____ so fast that _____.

3. These satellites make it possible for an event to be seen on television.

    a. The Internet makes it possible for _____.

    b. _____ makes it possible for _____.

4. They seem to be always in the same place in the sky.

    a. They seem to _____.

    b. _____ seem to _____.

5. Most of these satellites travel at the same speed as the Earth.

    a. _____ at the same speed as the train.

    b. _____ at the same _____ as _____.

Speaking Activities

Dialogue

Find a partner to practice the following dialogue.

A: Have you ever heard about communications satellites?

B: No, never. And you?

A: Of course, I have. Communications satellites make it possible for an event to be seen on TV everywhere.

B: How do you know that?

A: I read an article on the satellites in a magazine.

B: Any more information about the satellites?

A: Yes, there are three satellites being used by Asian countries now.

B: No wonder we can see news immediately no matter where we are.

A: Besides, communications satellites can transmit signals almost instantaneously.

B: Wow, can we find them in the sky?

A: That's impossible. They are sent high into the space by rockets.

B: Gosh! I sound stupid, don't I?

 *Listening Activities*

Sentence Comprehension

If the sentence you hear on tape means the same as the one you read below, put "S" in the blank; if not, put "D" in the blank.

_____ 1. Satellite communication happens so fast that it is almost instantaneous.

_____ 2. Because of these satellites, communication can be easy and rapid.

_____ 3. Telephone calls between any two places on Earth are now possible.

_____ 4. Stations on the ground, called Earth stations, send signals to these satellites.

_____ 5. Most of these satellites travel at the same speed as the Earth.

Sentence Dictation

Listen to the tape and fill in the blanks with the missing words.

1. Like a person looking in a _____, the returning signal was a _____ of the first signal.

2. _____ satellites are all active _____.

3. As these satellites circle the Earth, _____ are sent to them with _____ _____.

4. Satellite communication _____ so fast that it is almost _____.

5. Like the _____, communications satellites travel in a great _____ around our planet.

Sentence Memory

Listen to the sentences on tape. If the two sentences you hear mean the same, put "S" in the blank; if not, put "D" in the blank.

1. _____   2. _____   3. _____   4. _____   5. _____

Listen and Answer

Listen to the narrations and questions on tape. Then answer the questions by completing the following sentences.

1. Because there are _____.

2. They can be sure _____.

3. Because _____ the Earth.

4. They are usually _____ miles, or _____ kilo-

    meters _____.

5. Because _____ above the Earth _____.

Dialogue Comprehension

Listen to the dialogue on tape, and then answer the questions by completing the following sentences.

1. They were like _____.

2. The first ones were like _____. So messages

    _____.

3. They _____, amplify _____, and _____

    _____.

4. _____.

5. They can carry _____ at one time.

Writing Activities

Sentence Completion

Use your own words to complete the following.

1. High above the Earth, there are _____.

2. The first communications satellites were _____.

3. They receive the signals, amplify or _____.

4. As these satellites circle the Earth, messages _____.

5. A message can go up and down as many times as necessary to _____

_____.

Sentence Scrambling

Re-arrange the given chunks of words to form grammatical sentences.

1. carry/to relay/equipment/they/the signals

→ _____

2. messages/a ball on a road/bounced off/the satellites/like

→ _____

3. radio signals/waves/in straight lines/like/travel

→ _____

4. will continue/technicians/are sure/that/the messages

→ _____

5. satellite communication/fast/so...that/instantaneous/it's/happens/almost

→ _____

Translation

Translate the following Chinese sentences into English.

1. 大多數的人造衛星以和地球相同的速度運行。

   Most of these satellites travel _____ _____ _____ _____ as the Earth.

2. 有了這些人造衛星，通訊可以是容易且迅速的。

   _____ these satellites, _____ can be easy and rapid.

3. 在大西洋上方的通訊人造衛星，可以在同一個時間內傳送超過三萬通的電話。

   The communications satellites _____ the Atlantic Ocean can _____ more than 30,000 telephone _____ at _____ _____.

4. 音波以直線方式往上傳送到人造衛星，然後又以直線方式往下傳回到地球。

   The sound waves _____ in _____ _____ _____ up to a satellite and then in a straight line _____ to the Earth.

5. 因此，若有三個人造衛星分佈在適當的地方，訊息就可以傳遞到地球上的每個地方。

   Therefore, _____ three satellites in the _____ places, messages can go _____ on Earth.

Error Correction

In the following passage, some underlined parts are grammatically incorrect and some are not. Correct the errors, or put "○" in the blank if the underlined part is correct.

Answers:

The first communications satellites (1) <u>are like</u> sound or signal mirrors. Like a person (2) <u>looked</u> in a mirror, the returning signal was a reflection of the first signal. Messages (3) <u>bounced off</u> the satellite like a ball on a road. Today, however, communications satellites are all (4) <u>active device</u>. They receive the signals, amplify or strengthen them, and then (5) <u>relayed</u> them. The communications satellites over the Atlantic Ocean can carry (6) <u>more than</u> 30,000 telephone calls at one time.

(1) _____   (2) _____   (3) _____

(4) _____   (5) _____   (6) _____

Culture Shock

 Pre-reading Activities

Recognize New Words

Learn the Chinese definition of each bold-faced word in the following before you read the text.

    1. culture **shock**   衝擊

    2. specialist in **counseling**   諮詢

    3. **intercultural** studies   文化間的

    4. **adjust to** life   適應

5. three **stages**   階段

6. **obvious** reasons   明顯的

7. **self-conscious**   怕難為情的

8. **established positions**   已建立的身份地位

9. without an **identity**   身份

10. a feeling of **disorientation**   失落

11. create an **escape**   逃避現實的方法

12. a sense of **security**   安全

13. **familiarize** the person **with** the culture   使熟悉

14. **familiarity** and experience   熟悉

15. **solutions to** the problem   解決的辦法

Brainstorming Questions

Discuss the following questions with your group members.

1. What kind of emotional disturbance may be caused by culture shock?

2. How do you feel about cultural differences?

3. When you feel uneasy about a different culture, what do you do?

Read the Text

Living in a new country is not always wonderful and exciting. Culture shock is the feeling that people experience when they come to a new environment. Specialists in counseling and intercultural studies say that it is not easy to adjust to life in a new culture.

According to the specialists, there are three stages of culture shock. First, the newcomers like the environment. Then, they

5

begin to hate the new culture when the newness disappears. Finally, they begin to adjust themselves to the environment and enjoy their lives more.   10

Here are some of the obvious reasons for culture shock, such as the unpleasant weather, the different customs, the public service system difficult to them and the strange food. Moreover, if you don't look similar to the natives, you may feel strange. You may feel like everyone is watching you. In fact, you are always   15 watching yourself. You are self-conscious.

Everyone experiences culture shock in some form or another. But culture shock comes as a surprise to most people. Very often the people with the worst culture shock are the people who never had any difficulties in their own countries. When they   20 come to a new country, they do not have the same established positions or hobbies. They find themselves without a role, almost without an identity. They have to build a new self-image.

Culture shock produces a feeling of disorientation. When people feel the disorientation of culture shock, they sometimes   25 feel like staying inside all the time. They want to protect themselves from the unfamiliar environment. They want to create an escape within their rooms to give themselves a sense of security. This escape does solve the problem of culture shock for the short term, but it does nothing to familiarize the person more   30 with the culture. Familiarity and experience are the long-term solutions to the problem of culture shock.

Reading Comprehension Check

According to the text you read, choose the best answer to each question.

( ) 1. What is the main topic of the article?

(A) It is necessary to study different cultures.

(B) It describes what culture shock is like.

(C) Culture shock produces complicated disorientation.

(D) Everyone experiences culture shock in some form or another.

( ) 2. Which of the following is not an obvious cause of culture shock?

(A) Unpleasant weather.   (B) Different customs.

(C) Strange food.   (D) Different family system.

( ) 3. According to the article, which is the second stage of culture shock?

(A) The newcomers like the environment.

(B) The newcomers feel exciting and happy.

(C) The newcomers hate the new culture when the newness disappears.

(D) The newcomers adjust themselves to the environment and enjoy their lives more.

( ) 4. Who may be likely to experience culture shock?

(A) Everyone.   (B) Immigrants.

(C) Newcomers.   (D) Foreign students.

( ) 5. If people feel the disorientation of culture shock, what might they do?

(A) They often make mistakes of all kinds.

(B) They feel like staying inside all the time.

(C) They don't want to protect themselves.

(D) They may make an escape from home.

( ) 6. Culture shock is _____.

(A) the feeling that immigrants experience when they come to a new country

(B) the feeling of being frightened because of different ways of doing things

(C) a nightmare some people may have when they travel to a new country

(D) an environmental problem which newcomers cannot get used to

(   ) 7. You may feel like everyone is watching you because _____.

(A) you are so attractive

(B) the unpleasant weather makes you uneasy

(C) you do not dress the same way as the local people

(D) you are always watching yourself

(   ) 8. What kind of people may have the worst culture shock?

(A) Those who never had any difficulties in their own countries.

(B) Those who don't like other cultures.

(C) Those who are immature and less experienced.

(D) Those who don't have cultural background.

(   ) 9. Culture shock produces _____.

(A) a feeling of disorientation   (B) in different forms

(C) a feeling of happiness   (D) a feeling of hunger

(   ) 10. How do people who have culture shock behave?

(A) They have established social positions and hobbies.

(B) They find themselves without a role.

(C) They create an escape so as to achieve a sense of security.

(D) They have to build a new self-image.

Cloze Test

Fill in each blank with a proper word.

Living in a new country is not always ____1____ and exciting. Culture

shock is the ____2____ that people experience when they come to a new
____3____. Specialists in counseling and intercultural studies say that it is not
easy to ____4____ to life in a new culture.

( )   1. (A) troublesome   (B) incredible   (C) wonderful   (D) enormous
( )   2. (A) sense   (B) thinking   (C) situation   (D) feeling
( )   3. (A) style   (B) environment   (C) fashion   (D) atmosphere
( )   4. (A) adjust   (B) accustom   (C) apt   (D) adapt

According to the specialists, there are three stages of culture shock. First, the
newcomers like the environment. ____5____, they begin to hate the new culture
when the ____6____ disappears. Finally, they begin to ____7____ themselves to
the environment and enjoy their lives more.

Here are some of the obvious reasons for culture shock, ____8____ the
____9____ weather, the different customs, and the public service system difficult
to them. Moreover, if you don't look similar to the ____10____, you may feel
strange. You may feel like everyone ____11____ you. ____12____, you are always
watching yourself. You are self-conscious.

( )   5. (A) Accordingly   (B) Then   (C) So   (D) Nevertheless
( )   6. (A) friends   (B) children   (C) newness   (D) loneliness
( )   7. (A) adopt   (B) adapt   (C) adjust   (D) accord
( )   8. (A) due to   (B) because of   (C) such as   (D) so that
( )   9. (A) pleased   (B) pleasant   (C) unpleasant   (D) friendly
( ) 10. (A) natives   (B) visitors   (C) tourists   (D) newcomers
( ) 11. (A) is watching   (B) watches   (C) is to watch   (D) watching
( ) 12. (A) In fact   (B) As a result   (C) Hence   (D) Finally

Everyone experiences culture shock ____13____. But culture shock comes

_____14_____ to most people. A lot of the time, the people _____15_____ the worst culture shock are the people who never had any difficulties _____16_____ their own countries. _____17_____ they come to a new country, they do not have the same established positions or hobbies. They find themselves _____18_____ a role, almost without a(n) _____19_____. And especially when people feel the disorientation of culture shock, they sometimes feel like staying _____20_____ all the time. They want to protect themselves from the unfamiliar environment.

( ) 13. (A) in some form or another　(B) in a form or the other

　　　　(C) in one form or the other　(D) in the other forms

( ) 14. (A) as a surprise　(B) naturally　(C) like a luck　(D) unexpectedly

( ) 15. (A) with　(B) from　(C) by　(D) of

( ) 16. (A) from　(B) with　(C) in　(D) of

( ) 17. (A) When　(B) So　(C) Because　(D) Although

( ) 18. (A) having　(B) without　(C) lack　(D) in want

( ) 19. (A) identity　(B) significance　(C) characteristic　(D) image

( ) 20. (A) inside　(B) abroad　(C) outside　(D) loneliness

Correction

According to the text you read, correct the errors in the following sentences to make them grammatically correct and meaningful. Underline your corrections.

1. The reason why people have culture shock is that want to protect themselves from the familiar environment.

   _____

2. Two long-term solutions to the problem of culture shock are familiar and experience.

   _____

3. People with the worst culture shock are the people who already had many

difficulties in their own countries.

_____

4. It is so difficult to adjust to life in a new culture.

_____

5. Newcomers begin to hate the new culture when the homesickness appears.

_____

Developing Linguistic Ability

Morphology

> In English, a prefix can be added to the beginning of a word in order to form a different word. Take the prefixes '**dis-**' and '**un-**' which means '**not**' for example.

Examples:

1: **Disorientation** is formed by adding the prefix 'dis-' which means 'not' to the word, 'orientation.' dis- + orientation → disorientation

2: **Unfamiliar** is formed by adding the prefix 'un-' which means 'not' to the word, 'familiar.' un- + familiar → unfamiliar

Give one antonym to each of the following words.

1. appear → _____

2. happy → _____

3. advantage → _____

4. fortunate → _____

5. agree → _____

6. lucky → _____

7. approve → _____

8. comfortable → _____

9. like → _____

10. conscious → _____

Structure Imitation

Follow the given structure to create your own sentences.

1. Culture shock comes as a surprise to most people.

   → _____ comes as a _____ to _____.

2. People with the worst culture shock are the ones who never had any difficulties in their own countries.

   → Students with _____ are the ones who _____.

3. They find themselves without a role, almost without an identity.

   → Homeless people find themselves without _____, almost without _____.

4. Culture shock produces a feeling of disorientation.

   → _____ produces a feeling of _____.

5. They want to protect themselves from the unfamiliar environment.

   → _____ want to protect _____ from _____

   _____.

Grammar Focus — Idiomatic Phrases

> In English, some verbs and adjectives have to be followed by the preposition 'to.'

Example:

1. **adjust to** life in a new culture

The verb 'adjust' has to be followed by either 'oneself' or 'to' which takes an object.

→ They *adjust themselves* very well and very fast.

→ They have to *adjust to* the new environment.

2. look **similar to** the natives

The adjective 'similar' has to be followed by the preposition 'to.'

→ This picture looks *similar to* me.

Follow the rule mentioned above to complete each of the following sentences.

1. This word does not look familiar _____ me.

2. These two boys look very similar _____ each other.

3. We have to adjust ourselves _____ the new life style.

4. Young people are quick to adapt _____ new circumstances.

5. Add a few more names _____ the list.

6. She owes her career as a singer _____ her parents.

7. Penicillin has contributed greatly _____ the welfare of mankind.

8. The engine of a car corresponds _____ the heart of a man.

9. A politician must appeal _____ public opinion to win the election.

10. Twice two is equal _____ four.

 Speaking Activities

Dialogue Practice

Find a partner to practice the following dialogue.

Frank is a student from Taiwan. He and Steve are studying in an American university now.

Steve: Hi, Frank. Are you OK? Why do you look so upset?

Frank: It's the weather. The cold weather upsets me.

Steve: Do you mean the weather is unpleasant?

Frank: Yes. You know, in southern Taiwan, I don't need to wear a sweater even in winter. Here's quite different. Now, it is October, but the temperature is so low that I have to wear a coat.

Steve: Yah, you are right. Here in North America, the weather is much colder.

Frank: You know, this is my fourth week here. When I first came here, everything seemed new and strange to me. I was quite excited. But, now, I feel upset about almost everything.

Steve: Don't worry! It's normal. When the newness disappears, you begin to hate the new environment.

Frank: Yes, you're right. I even don't know what I should wear. It also bothers me a lot.

Steve: Why?

Frank: My friends often laugh at the clothes I wear. They often say I look strange to them.

Steve: Never mind. You know, you are experiencing culture shock. Try to adjust yourself to the new environment. And you will be OK soon. Cheer up!

Group Discussion

Discuss the following questions with your group members. Then, report your answers to the class.

1. What are the three stages of culture shock?

2. How do most people react to culture shock?

3. When people have culture shock, what suggestions you may give to them?

4. Do people who experience culture shock have to see a doctor? Why or why not?

Dialogue Completion

Complete the following dialogue.

A: Hi, Betty. You look spest. What's up?

B: _____. I don't know what's wrong with myself.

A: Does the weather bother you?

B: Yes. I think so. I am not _____.

A: Here, in winter, the temperature often drops down to zero.

B: No wonder I always feel _____.

A: What _____ bothers you?

B: The food.

A: What's _____ with the food?

B: Here people have cold food most of the time. I am not _____.

A: Don't worry about it. I had had the same problem, too. But I am OK now.

B: Do I need to see a doctor?

A: No. You are just having _____. Once you adjust _____ well, you will be all right.

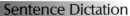

Listening Activities

Sentence Dictation

Listen to the tape, and fill in the blanks with missing words.

1. Living in a foreign country is not always _____.

2. The second stage of culture shock is that people begin to _____
_____.

3. When you realize that you are different from the natives, you feel _____ about _____.

4. People may find themselves without _____ in a foreign country.

5. People who have the worst culture shock are those who never _____
_____.

6. A feeling of _____ is caused by culture shock.

7. People would like to create an escape within their rooms with a hope to give themselves _____.

8. _____ are the long-term solutions to the problem of culture shock.

9. Culture shock comes as _____ to most people.

10. Culture shock is a _____ that people experience when they go to a foreign country.

Sentence Memory

Listen to the sentences on tape. If the two sentences you hear mean the same, put "S" in the blank; if not, put "D" in the blank.

1. _____   2. _____   3. _____   4. _____   5. _____

Writing Activities

Sentence Scrambling

Re-arrange the given chunks to make meaningful sentences.

1. of disorientation/culture shock/a feeling/produces

2. with the worst/are/the people/had any difficulties/the people/who never/in their /culture shock/own countries

_____

3. the long-term/familiarity/culture shock/and experience/are/solutions to/the problem of

_____

4. without/they find/almost without/an identity/themselves/a role

_____

5. is not/and exciting/living/always/in a/wonderful/new country

_____

Error Correction

In the following passage, some underlined parts are grammatically incorrect and some are not. Correct the errors, or put "○" in the blank if the underlined part is correct.

> Everyone experiences (1) culture shocks in (2) some forms or other. But (3) they comes (4) like a surprise to most people. (5) A lot of times, (6) the people of the worst culture shock (7) are the one who never (8) have much difficulties in their own (9) country. When they (10) came to a (11) new countries, they do not have (12) same establishing positions or hobbies. They find (13) themselves without a role, almost without (14) an identification. They have to build a new (15) self-imagination.

Answers:

(1) _____ (2) _____ (3) _____

(4) _____ (5) _____ (6) _____

(7) _____   (8) _____   (9) _____

(10) _____   (11) _____   (12) _____

(13) _____   (14) _____   (15) _____

Free Writing

Write down three ways that you think of to solve the problem of culture shock.

1. _____

2. _____

3. _____

Unit Five

Procrastination

 Pre-reading Activities

Recognize New Words

Learn the Chinese definition of each bold-faced word in the following before you read the text.

    1. **procrastinate**   耽擱

    2. to **postpone** until tomorrow   拖延

    3. **delay** doing something   耽擱

    4. **put off** what they should do   拖延

5. have a **tendency**	傾向；趨勢
6. **miss deadlines**	錯過截止日期
7. **rarely** procrastinate	很少
8. highly **efficient**	有效率的
9. well-**organized** people	有條理的
10. I **suspect** that...	覺得…可能
11. a daily **schedule**	進度表；行程表
12. be **reasonable**	合理的
13. **crowd** the list **with** tasks	擠滿
14. be **lenient** with ourselves	寬容的
15. get **discouraged**	洩氣的

Brainstorming Questions

Discuss the following questions with your group members.

1. Have you ever missed the deadline of handing in your homework? Why?

2. Describe a procrastinator.

3. If you have a habit of procrastination, how will you overcome it?

4. What disadvantages of being a procrastinator can you think of?

5. Find a book on time management. Give a summary report. Tell who the author is and what his suggestions are?

Read the Text

The verb procrastinate comes from the Latin procrastinare, which means "to postpone until tomorrow." Procrastinating is delaying doing something until some future time. Procrastinators are always putting off what they should be doing right now.

Those of us who have a tendency toward procrastination   5
know that it is a terrible habit. Every day, we tell ourselves to start
doing things immediately; however, we procrastinate our work,
miss deadlines, and break promises. Because we always procrastinate, we are always trying to catch up. We are always
doing yesterday's jobs today, and today's jobs tomorrow.   10

There are people who rarely procrastinate. They are highly
efficient and well-organized people. They seem to get everything
done on time. I suspect that they never leave home in the
morning before they make the bed, never go to sleep at night
before they finish their work, and are never late for appointments.   15
As a result, they are probably always one step ahead of you and
me.

Maybe the way to overcome procrastination is to change
ourselves gradually. We can start with a daily schedule of the
things we need to accomplish. But let's be reasonable. We   20
shouldn't crowd the list with too many tasks. We should be
realistic about what we can do. Especially in the beginning, we
should be lenient with ourselves. After all, if we fail at the start,
we will get discouraged and go right back to our old habits.

Reading Comprehension Check I

According to the text you read, choose the best answer to each question.

(   ) 1. What does the word "procrastinate" mean?

(A) To do things in advance.   (B) To postpone until tomorrow.

(C) To finish something completely.   (D) To draw a plan well.

(   ) 2. Where does the word "procrastinate" come from?

     (A) Greek.   (B) Roman.   (C) Latin.   (D) Japanese.

(   ) 3. A procrastinator is one who _____.

     (A) does his or her job incompletely   (B) plans things in advance

     (C) asks for others' help   (D) delays doing things until some future time

(   ) 4. Which of the following is a possible way to overcome procrastination?

     (A) To change it gradually.   (B) To change it rapidly.

     (C) To give it up right away.   (D) To ignore it completely.

(   ) 5. If we fail at the start to overcome the habit of procrastination, we will

     _____.

     (A) be very happy and joyful

     (B) get discouraged and go right back to the old habit

     (C) neglect it and be confident of success

     (D) do it again and won't care about it

Reading Comprehension Check II

According to the text you read, put "T" in the blank if the statement is true; put
"F" if it is not.

(   ) 1. The verb *procrastinate* comes from the French *procrastinare*, which
     means "to hurry up."

(   ) 2. Every day, we tell ourselves that we must start doing things at once but
     we usually fail.

(   ) 3. Most of people are always doing tomorrow's jobs today and today's jobs
     yesterday.

(   ) 4. People who rarely procrastinate are probably always one step ahead of
     you and me.

(   ) 5. According to the text, when we make plans to break bad habits, we should be lenient with ourselves in the beginning.

Reading and Writing

According to the text you read, answer the following questions by completing the sentences below.

1. Do you usually delay doing something until some future time?

   Yes, I usually delay _____.

   No, I seldom delay _____.

2. If you are a procrastinator, how can you break the habit? If you never procrastinate, how do you make it?

   I will break the habit by _____.

   I make it by _____.

3. Do you think it is good for you to get everything done on time?

   Yes, I think it is _____.

4. Why shouldn't we crowd the list with too many tasks?

   Because if _____, probably we _____

   _____.

5. Should we be lenient with ourselves in the beginning when making a plan? Why or why not?

   Yes, we should be _____ because if we

   _____.

Reading Analysis

Write down the topic sentence of each paragraph in the text you read.

1. Paragraph 1: _____

2. Paragraph 2: _____

3. Paragraph 3: _____

4. Paragraph 4: _____

5. The main idea of the text: _____

Interpreting the Text

According to the text you read, answer the following questions by completing the sentences below.

1. In paragraph 1, what does "procrastinate" mean?

   It means _____.

2. What is the main idea of paragraph 1?

   It explains what _____.

3. Procrastination is a bad habit. Why?

   That's because it makes you postpone _____, _____

   _____, and break _____.

4. In paragraph 3, how do we describe people who rarely procrastinate?

   They are _____.

5. In paragraph 3, why are people who rarely procrastinate always one step ahead
   of us?

   That's because they _____.

6. In paragraph 4, what's the best way to overcome procrastination?

   That is to _____.

7. In paragraph 4, why should we be realistic and lenient with ourselves while
   making a plan to overcome procrastination?

   That's because if _____.

8. In paragraph 4, why shouldn't we crowd our schedule with too many tasks?

   That's because if we do, we _____.

Error Correction

According to the text you read, find the errors in the following sentences to make them grammatically correct and meaningful. Underline your corrections.

1. The verb *procrastinate* comes from the Greek origin *procrastinare*.

_____

2. Procrastinating is doing things until some future time.

_____

3. People who have a tendency toward procrastination know it a study skill.

_____

4. We are always doing tomorrow's jobs today, and today's jobs yesterday.

_____

5. There are highly efficient and well-organized people who always procrastinate and seem to get everything unfinished on time.

_____

Cloze Test

According to the text you read, fill in the blanks with the missing words.

I suspect that those people never leave home in the morning before making the bed, never go to sleep at night before finishing their work, and are never late for appointments. Therefore, they are probably always one step a_____d of us. Maybe the way to o_____e procrastination is to c_____e ourselves gradually. We can start w_____h a daily schedule of the things we need to a_____h. But be reasonable. We shouldn't crowd the l_____t with too many tasks. We should be realistic about w_____t we can do. Especially in the beginning, we should be l_____t with ourselves. A_____r all, if we fail at the start, we will get d_____d and go right back to our old habits.

Developing Linguistic Ability

Word Definition

Match each of the words in the left column with its definition given in the right column.

Words

_____ 1. procrastinate
_____ 2. tendency
_____ 3. efficient
_____ 4. deadline
_____ 5. rarely
_____ 6. organize
_____ 7. suspect
_____ 8. schedule
_____ 9. reasonable
_____ 10. lenient

Definitions

(A) not severe or strict
(B) working well, quickly, and without waste
(C) sensible, rational
(D) a timetable of things to be done
(E) to think likely
(F) to make necessary arrangements for something
(G) not often
(H) a date or time before which something must be done
(I) to put off, delay
(J) a natural likelihood, trend

Cloze Test

Fill in each blank with one of the words given. Make some changes, if necessary.

procrastinator	tendency	efficient	schedule
organized	reasonable	postpone	deadline
suspect	delay	rarely	lenient

1. Car-pooling is an _____ way of saving energy.

2. The game was _____ until Friday afternoon because of rain.

3. It seems quite natural that the elders have the _____ to live in the past.

4. You are too _____ to your children. You're spoiling them.

5. Maria is a hopeless _____. She never gets her work done on time.

6. Work hard or we will miss the _____.

7. Try to be _____. How can I give you 20 dollars when I only have five?

8. Miracles _____ happen.

9. The teacher has a very tight _____. She always seems busy.

10. I _____ him to know the secret.

11. The ideas are _____ well in this report.

12. Procrastinators always _____ doing things until the last moment.

Vocabulary Development

Synonyms: Give one synonym to each of the following words.

1. procrastinate → _____

2. schedule → _____

3. crowd → _____

4. tendency → _____

5. reasonable → _____

6. lenient → _____

Antonyms: Give one antonym to each of the following words.

1. reasonable → _____

2. rarely → _____

3. discourage → _____

4. lenient → _____

5. efficient → _____

Morphology

I: The prefix 'in-,' 'im-,' or 'un-' means 'no/not.' Add one of them to each of the following words to form a different word.

1. realistic → _____

2. reasonable → _____

3. efficient → _____

4. organized → _____

5. done → _____

II: *Add the suffix '-tion' or '-ment' to each of the following words to form the noun.*

1. procrastinate → _____   4. discourage → _____

2. organize → _____   5. accomplish → _____

3. postpone → _____

Phrase in Use I

Choose the correct answers.

(　) 1. If it rains, the match must be _____.

    (A) put off　(B) turned down　(C) called upon　(D) switched on

(　) 2. When will Britain _____ Japan in industrial production?

    (A) catch up with　(B) brush up　(C) show up　(D) cover up

(　) 3. Do the trains ever run _____ here?

    (A) out of time　(B) from time to time　(C) on time　(D) over time

(　) 4. He was late _____ the snow.

    (A) by means of　(B) due to　(C) as a result from　(D) in the event of

(　) 5. Our income has got smaller, so we must be realistic and _____ our car.

    (A) hold up　(B) give up　(C) turn up　(D) show up

(　) 6. If people don't have enough time to finish their work, they may _____.

    (A) put it down　(B) put it away　(C) put it out　(D) put it off

(　) 7. Because we always procrastinate, we are always trying to _____.

    (A) worry about　(B) catch up　(C) complain about　(D) turn down

(　) 8. The festival _____ a huge firework display.

    (A) start with　(B) skip over　(C) leak out　(D) leave alone

(　) 9. The time in New York is three hours _____ the time in San

Francisco.

(A) late of   (B) early on   (C) ahead of   (D) of late

(   ) 10. You ought not to _____.

(A) break promises   (B) keep your words

(C) make promises   (D) keep promises

Phrase in Use II

Fill in each of the blanks with one of the words given. Make some changes, if necessary.

put off   catch up   on time   come from
ahead of   as a result   realistic about

1. He never paid much attention to the teacher in class. _____, he failed the exam.

2. If you don't finish your work today, you have to _____ tomorrow.

3. Don't _____ what you can do today till tomorrow.

4. If you are _____, you are not late.

5. Do you know where this passage _____?

Structure Focus

Follow the sentence structures given below to create your own sentences.

1. To procrastinate is to delay doing something until some future time.

a. To _____ is to _____.

b. To _____ is to _____.

2. They never go to sleep at night before they finish their work.

a. They never _____ before they _____.

b. _____ never _____ before _____

_____.

3. There are people who rarely procrastinate.

   a. There are _____ who rarely _____.

   b. There are _____ who _____.

4. Maybe the way to overcome procrastination is to change ourselves gradually.

   a. Maybe the way to _____ is to _____.

   b. Maybe the way to _____ is to _____.

5. Because we always procrastinate, we are always trying to catch up.

   a. Because we always _____ late, we are always _____

   _____.

   b. Because we always _____, we always _____

   _____.

Grammar Focus

In the following, you are going to learn about two-word verbs, also called **phrasal verbs**. What is a two-word verb? If a verb is always followed by a preposition or always used with a preposition, the verb is considered as a two-word verb.

Now tell which of the following is a two-word verb. Put a "○" in the blank before a two-word verb, and a "✕" if it is not.

_____ 1. call on a friend   _____ 4. ask you a question

_____ 2. come from Taiwan   _____ 5. put off the work

_____ 3. receive it with thanks   _____ 6. push the door apart

If a two-word verb can be separated, it is called a separable two-word verb. If it is not, it is called a non-separable two-word verb.

Tell which of the following is separable. Put "S" in the blank of a separable, and "N" in the blank of a non-separable.

_____ 1. The little boy put away his key.

_____ 2. Daniel put on his hat.

_____ 3. The street was covered up with snow.

_____ 4. She called off the meeting.

_____ 5. They asked for the teacher's help.

_____ 6. They got on the bus quickly.

Speaking Activities

Group Discussion

Discuss the following questions with your group members. Then, report your answers to the class.

1. How do you manage your time?

2. What should be taken into consideration when making a reasonable schedule?

3. What are the disadvantages of being a procrastinator? List at least five of them.

4. Who are current experts on time management? Name at least three popular authors who wrote books on time management.

5. What should we do to overcome procrastination?

Dialogue Completion

Invite a partner to practice the following dialogue. You play the part B, and your partner plays the part A. Change the role later on.

A: What bad habits do you have?

B: I have one terrible habit. That is _____.

A: How does it affect you?

B: It _____.

A: Do you want to break this bad habit?

B: Yes, but I don't know how. Do you know anyone who is a procrastinator, too?

A: Sure. _____.

B: Do you often put off what you should be doing right now?

A: Yes. Once in a while I _____.

B: What should we do to overcome procrastination?

A: _____.

B: That's a good idea!

Interview

Make an interview with one or two of your classmates and fill out the following form.

[Interview Sheet]

Interviewee's name: _____ **Sex:** _____ **Male** _____ **Female**
1. Do you usually miss the deadline of your homework?
☐ Yes.   ☐ No.
2. Do you often crowd your daily schedule with too many tasks?
☐ Yes, always.   ☐ Yes, sometimes.
☐ No, seldom.   ☐ No, never.
3. What do you think of your daily schedule?
☐ Very reasonable.   ☐ Sort of reasonable.
☐ Not reasonable.   ☐ Awfully tight.
4. Do you like to work with somebody who always postpone?
☐ Yes.   ☐ No.

5. Do you go to bed before you finish your homework?

☐ Yes, always.   ☐ Yes, sometimes.

☐ No, seldom.   ☐ No, never.

Dialogue Practice

Find a partner to practice the following dialogue.

A: Can you help me with my homework?

B: What? It's ten o'clock at night. Why didn't you do it earlier?

A: I just couldn't. I've been working on other assignments all day long.

B: But you should have told me earlier. Now, I am going to bed.

A: Oh, no! What should I do now? If I don't hand it in on time tomorrow, my teacher will blame me.

B: You know, you deserve it. You always repeat the same error. I have told you thousands of times, "Never put off what you should do today until tomorrow." It's time for you to learn some lessons and break such a terrible habit.

Listening Activities

Listen and Answer

Listen to the narrations and questions on tape. Then answer the questions by completing the following sentences.

1. The word "procrastinate" originates from _____.

2. To procrastinate is to _____.

3. Procrastination is a _____.

4. A procrastinator always tries to _____.

5. A procrastinator is always doing _____.

6. We can find some highly _____.

7. Because they never procrastinate their _____ every day.

8. We can change ourselves _____.

9. We shouldn't crowd the daily schedule _____.

10. It means we should not _____ at the beginning.

Dialogue Comprehension

Listen to the tape, and then fill in the blanks with the missing words.

Peter: God, I haven't finished my assignments yet, and tomorrow morning will be the _____. Would you please help me with them tonight, Amy?

Amy: Here you go again! Why didn't you start earlier?

Peter: I did, but I've been too busy. I planned to do lots of things during this summer vacation. I can hardly finish all of the assignments before the deadline.

Amy: So let's be reasonable. Don't crowd your _____ with too many tasks. Be _____!

Peter: I see. I'll turn over a new leaf tomorrow.

Sentence Memory

Listen to the sentences on tape. If the two sentences you hear mean the same, put "S" in the blank; if not, put "D" in the blank.

1. _____ 2. _____ 3. _____ 4. _____ 5. _____

Sentence Dictation

Listen to the tape, and then fill in the blanks with the missing words.

1. The verb _____ comes from the Latin word *procrastinare*, which

   means "to _____ until tomorrow."

2. Those of us who have a _____ toward _____ know that it

   is a terrible habit.

3. Every day we _____ our work, _____ deadlines, and

   _____ promises.

4. Maybe the way to _____ procrastination is to change ourselves

   _____.

5. We can start with a daily _____ of the things we need to

   _____.

Sentence Comprehension

If the sentence you hear on tape means the same as the one you read below, put
"S" in the blank; if not, put "D" in the blank.

_____ 1. I suspect that they never leave home in the morning before they make the
   bed.

_____ 2. As a result, they are probably always one step ahead of you and me.

_____ 3. We shouldn't crowd the list with too many tasks.

_____ 4. They are highly efficient and well-organized.

_____ 5. Those of us who have a tendency toward procrastination know that it is a
   terrible habit.

Writing Activities

Sentence Completion

Use your own words to complete the following sentences.

1. Every day, we tell ourselves that _____.

2. Maybe the way to overcome procrastination is _____.

3. We should be realistic about _____.

4. If we fail at the start, we will _____.

5. "Never put off until tomorrow" means _____.

Sentence Scrambling

Re-arrange the given chunks of words to form grammatical sentences.

1. our old habits/will go right back/after all/if /at the start/we/get discouraged/we fail/and/we/to

   → _____

2. in the beginning/ourselves/be lenient with/we should/especially

   → _____

3. the things/we/need to/can start/accomplish/we/a daily schedule/with/of

   → _____

4. of us/toward/that/know/those/it is/who have/a terrible habit/procrastination/a tendency

   → _____

5. probably/you and me/as a result/one step/ahead of/they are/always

   → _____

Guided Writing

Follow the hints to write a paragraph of about 80 words.

Topic: Never Put off What You Should Do Today until Tomorrow

(1)〔主題句〕People tend to delay doing things until tomorrow. (2)〔説明第一個原因〕（人們常常把今天應該做的事情拖延到第二天才做。）People often _____ what they should _____ until _____ _____. (3)（最常用的藉口是太忙。）The _____ is that they _____. (4)〔説明第二個原因〕（另一個可能的藉口是他們有太多的事情要做。）The another _____ is that they _____ _____ _____. (5)〔對拖延的習慣做一個評定〕（無論藉口是什麼，人們已經有了拖延的壞習慣。）No _____ the _____, people already have the _____ of _____. (6)〔説明有拖延習慣的人的弱點〕（有拖延習慣的人通常是今天做昨天的事，明天做今天的事。）People who have the _____ of _____ often do _____ today, and do _____ tomorrow. (7)（這就是為什麼他們有如此多的事情要做。）This is why they always _____. (8)〔再舉例説明拖延的弱點〕（他們不能遵守諾言，做事沒效率。）They can't _____ and _____ _____. (9)〔作結論句呼應題目〕（因此，我們不應該把今天可做的事情拖延到明天才做。）Therefore, we should not _____ _____.

Error Correction

In the following passage, some underlined parts are grammatically incorrect and some are not. Correct the errors, or put a "○" in the blank if the underlined part is correct.

> To procrastinate is (1) <u>delaying doing</u> something (2) <u>until</u> some future time. A procrastinator will always (3) <u>putting off</u> what they should be (4) <u>doing</u> right now till tomorrow. (5) <u>Procrastinating</u> is a terrible habit. Every day, procrastinators (6) <u>ourselves</u> that (7) <u>we</u> must start doing things right away. However, every day, they postpone (8) <u>our works</u>, (9) <u>miss the deadline</u>, and break promises. They are always doing yesterday's jobs today, and today's jobs tomorrow.

Answers:

(1) _____ (2) _____ (3) _____

(4) _____ (5) _____ (6) _____

(7) _____ (8) _____ (9) _____

Free Writing

Write down at least five disadvantages of being a procrastinator.

The disadvantages of being a procrastinator can be plenty. In my opinions there are five major disadvantages of procrastination. First, _____ _____. Second, _____ _____. Third, _____ ___. The fourth disadvantage is that _____ _____. The last but not the least is that _____ _____. To conclude, being a procrastinator is _____ _____.

Translation I

Translate the following Chinese sentences into English.

1. 絕對不要把你今天應該做的事拖到明天才做。

_____

2. 如果我們把今天的工作拖到明天，那麼我們會把明天的工作拖到後天。

_____

3. 結果，我們每天就會有太多事情要做。

_____

4. 拖延是一種壞習慣。

_____

5. 有拖延習慣的人做事沒有效率。

_____

6. 有拖延習慣的人很容易失去成功的良機。

_____

Translation II

Translate the following Chinese sentences into English.

1. 每天，我們告訴自己必須立刻做事情。

   Every day, we tell ourselves that we must do _____ _____.

2. 也許克服延宕的方法就是漸進地改變我們自己。

   Maybe the way to _____ _____ is to change ourselves gradually.

3. 他們似乎準時地做每件事。

   They seem to get everything _____ _____ _____.

4. 很少拖延的人們是很有效率和很有計畫的。

   People who _____ procrastinate are _____ efficient and well-organized.

5. 特別在剛開始時，我們應該對自己寬大。

   Especially _____ _____ _____, we should be _____ with ourselves.

Unit Six

Healthwatch: How Much Exercise Do We Really Need?

 Pre-reading Activities

Recognize New Words

Learn the Chinese definition of each bold-faced word in the following before you read the text.

    1. **be committed to**   投入於⋯

    2. **workouts**   身體的鍛鍊

    3. **vigorous** exercise   劇烈的

    4. **alternate** A **with** B   A 與 B 交互進行

5. **aerobics** classes	有氧運動
6. believe in the **motto**	箴言
7. **commercial**	以播放廣告為收入的節目
8. **overwhelming**	無法抵抗的
9. an **athlete**	運動員
10. **immune system**	免疫系統
11. **conjure up...**	使人想起…
12. **strenuous** activity	費勁的
13. health **benefits**	益處；利益
14. the new **guidelines**	指導方針
15. **moderate** activity	適度的
16. **be broken down into...**	被分成…
17. smaller **segments**	部分
18. **boost** your **metabolism**	促進新陳代謝
19. **work off** calories	消耗
20. **vending machine**	販賣機
21. **appeal to** you	吸引
22. **be serious about** exercise	對…認真

Brainstorming Questions

Discuss the following questions with your group members.

1. Why is exercise important to everybody?

2. How much exercise do we really need?

3. How to form the habit of doing exercise everyday?

Read the Text

Ellen and David are committed to their workouts at the health club. They both go every day after work and spend at least one hour doing vigorous exercise, alternating tough aerobics classes with working out on the machines and lifting weights. Both are in shape and feel fit. They believe in the motto, 5 "No pains, no gains."

Andy and Pam are sitting in front of the television and watching yet another commercial for the local gym. It all seems overwhelming—going to the gym, working up a sweat, and even finding the time. Neither one is an athlete, nor do they really care 10 to learn a sport now.

Are you more like Ellen and David or Andy and Pam? Or do you fall somewhere in between? We all know that exercise is important in keeping the body healthy and reducing the risks of disease. It also cuts down on stress and protects the body's 15 immune system. But for many people, the word exercise conjures up hours of boring, strenuous activity. Recently, however, scientific studies have found that health benefits can be achieved with non-strenuous exercise.

This is very encouraging news for all those people who 20 thought they had to be athletes or work as hard as athletes to make exercise worth it. The new guidelines say that every adult should do at least 30 minutes of moderate activity most days of the week. And these 30 minutes can even be broken down into

smaller segments during the day. The important thing is to be   25
consistent and make exercise part of your daily life.

  There are many ways to achieve this without buying
expensive equipment or joining a health club. Walking is one of
the best ways to get exercise. Try to go for a walk after lunch or
dinner to boost your metabolism and work off some calories. If   30
possible, walk all or part of the way to work or school. Use the
stairs instead of the elevator whenever you can. Gardening,
raking leaves, and dancing are also good activities. (However,
walking to the coffee or vending machine doesn't count!) As for
sports, even if tennis or golf doesn't appeal to you, hiking and   35
cycling can be relaxing and beneficial, too.

  Remember, you can be serious about exercise without taking it too seriously!

Reading Comprehension Check

*I: According to the text you read, if the statements in the following are true, put
"T" in the blank; if not, put "F" in the blank.*

(   ) 1. Andy and Pam are committed to their workouts at the health club.

(   ) 2. Scientific studies have found that health benefits can be achieved with
non-strenuous exercise.

(   ) 3. Exercise is not important in keeping the body healthy and reducing the
risks of disease.

(   ) 4. Every adult should do at least 30 minutes of moderate activity most days
of the week.

(   ) 5. Walking is one of the best ways to get exercise.

II: According to the text you read, answer the following questions by completing the sentences below.

1. How much time do Ellen and David spend at the health club every day?

   They spend at least _____ at the health club every day.

2. Why is exercise important?

   Exercise is important in _____.

3. What is one of the best ways to get exercise?

   _____ is one of the best ways to get exercise.

4. How do people think of the word exercise?

   For many people, the word "exercise" conjures up _____

   _____.

5. If tennis or golf doesn't appeal to you, what kind of exercise can be relaxing and beneficial?

   _____ can be also relaxing and beneficial.

III: According to the text you read, choose the best answer to each of the following questions.

(   ) 1. What kind of sports can be relaxing and beneficial?

   (A) Hiking.   (B) Tennis.   (C) Aerobics.   (D) Golf.

(   ) 2. How much time is suitable for adults to make exercise every day?

   (A) 30 minutes.   (B) 60 minutes.   (C) 10 minutes.   (D) 2 hours.

(   ) 3. Which of the following mottos do Ellen and David believe?

   (A) A bad thing never dies.   (B) Beauty is only skin deep.

   (C) No pains, no gains.   (D) Don't wash your dirty linen in public.

(   ) 4. What can help you stay healthy and protect your body's immune system?

   (A) Drinking a cup of coffee.   (B) Walking to work.

   (C) Watching TV.   (D) Eating junk food.

(   ) 5. For what purpose do people go for a walk after lunch or dinner?

    (A) Work off some calories.

    (B) Appreciate the beautiful sight.

    (C) Remember what happened during the day.

    (D) Make themselves look beautiful.

Developing Linguistic Ability

Vocabulary Definition

Match the word in the left column with the proper definition given in the right column.

_____ 1. motto

_____ 2. conjure

_____ 3. metabolism

_____ 4. strenuous

_____ 5. athlete

_____ 6. vigorous

_____ 7. commercial

_____ 8. benefit

_____ 9. moderate

_____10. commit

(A) one who practices bodily exercises and games that need strength and speed

(B) strong, forceful

(C) an adventage

(D) to bring into mind

(E) a sentence or a few words taken as the principle of a person

(F) neither large nor small, high nor low, fast nor slow, etc.

(G) the chemical activities in a living thing by which it gains power, especially from food

(H) requiring great effort

(I) to promise (oneself, one's property, etc.) to a certain course of action

(J) an advertisement on television or radio

Vocabulary in Use

Choose the correct answers.

(　　) 1. Give your upper body a _____ by using dumbbells.

　　　　(A) printout　(B) handout　(C) workout　(D) dropout

(　　) 2. Very _____ exercise can increase the risk of heart attacks.

　　　　(A) vigorous　(B) moderate　(C) overwhelming　(D) generous

(　　) 3. My life _____ between work and sleep.

　　　　(A) commites　(B) discharges　(C) originates　(D) alternates

(　　) 4. I'd like to join a(n) _____ class to improve my fitness.

　　　　(A) aerobics　(B) history　(C) reading　(D) writing

(　　) 5. My _____ is "Never give up."

　　　　(A) memo　(B) motto　(C) menu　(D) photo

(　　) 6. Avoid _____ exercise in the evening.

　　　　(A) moderate　(B) nervous　(C) strenuous　(D) dull

(　　) 7. She doesn't get many _____ from this course.

　　　　(A) owners　(B) workouts　(C) benefits　(D) credits

(　　) 8. The _____ won two gold medals in the Olympics.

　　　　(A) ethnic　(B) ethics　(C) sports　(D) athlete

(　　) 9. The government has issued the _____ on the content of elementary education.

　　　　(A) permission　(B) admission　(C) headlines　(D) guidelines

(　　) 10. This policy will affect large _____ of the population.

　　　　(A) segments　(B) parliaments　(C) elements　(D) treatments

Vocabulary Development

Synonyms: Give one proper synonym to each of the following words.

1. segment → _____   4. benefit → _____

2. motto → _____

3. vigorous → _____

5. athlete → _____

6. moderate → _____

Antonyms: Give one antonym to each of the following words.

1. strenuous → _____

2. moderate → _____

3. segment → _____

4. reduce → _____

5. benefit → _____

Morphology

The prefix 'in-,' 'im-' or 'un-' means 'no/not.' Add one of them to each of the following words to form a different word.

1. expensive → _____

2. fit → _____

3. consistent → _____

4. possible → _____

5. healthy → _____

Add the suffix '-tion' or '-ment' to each of the following words to form the noun.

1. commit → _____

2. alternate → _____

3. achieve → _____

4. encourage → _____

5. moderate → _____

6. agree → _____

Idioms & Phrases

Match each of the phrases in the left column with its proper words in the right column.

_____ 1. break down   (A) to increase

_____ 2. be committed to (B) to treat as important

_____ 3. work off   (C) to remove, by work or activity

_____ 4. alternate...with... (D) reduce to pieces

_____ 5. conjure up   (E) to follow by turns

_____ 6. appeal to   (F) to cause to be remembered

_____ 7. be serious about   (G) to be dedicated to

                              (H) to be attractive to

Phrase in Use

Choose the correct answers.

(   ) 1. Ellen and David _____ their workouts at the health club.

(A) are given to   (B) are broken to

(C) are committed to   (D) are limited to

(   ) 2. Andy and Pam are sitting _____ the television and watching yet another commercial for the local gym.

(A) in the middle of   (B) in the front of   (C) in front of   (D) in back of

(   ) 3. For many people, the word "exercise" _____ hours of boring, strenuous activity.

(A) conjures up   (B) conjures away

(C) conjures down   (D) conjures above

(   ) 4. Use the stairs _____ the elevator whenever you can.

(A) take place   (B) instead of   (C) substitute for   (D) be replaced

(   ) 5. As for sports, _____ tennis or golf doesn't appeal to you, hiking and cycling can be relaxing and beneficial, too.

(A) even up   (B) even so   (C) even if   (D) and even

(   ) 6. Remember, you can _____ exercise without taking it too seriously.

(A) be neglected about   (B) take easy to

(C) disregard about   (D) be serious about

(   ) 7. The new guidelines say that every adult should do _____ 30 minutes of moderate activity most days of the week.

(A) at last   (B) at least   (C) at large   (D) at all

( ) 8. Modern art does _____ me.

(A) appeal to   (B) conjure up   (C) commit to   (D) appeal against

( ) 9. Miss Lin _____ her excess fat by doing exercise.

(A) works out   (B) works away   (C) works off   (D) works on

( ) 10. The glass fell and _____ pieces.

(A) broke down   (B) broke down into   (C) broke into   (D) broke with

Structure Focus

Follow the sentence structures given below to create your own sentences.

1. Neither one is an athlete, nor do they really care to learn a sport now.

 a. Neither _____ nor _____.

 b. Neither _____ nor _____ is an athlete.

2. We all know that exercise is important in keeping the body healthy.

 a. We all know that _____ important in _____ _____.

 b. We know that _____ are important to _____ _____.

3. The important thing is to be consistent and make exercise part of your daily life.

 a. The important thing is to be _____ and _____ _____ every day.

 b. The important thing is to _____ and _____ _____ in class.

4. Walking is one of the best ways to get exercise.

 a. _____ is one of the best ways to _____.

 b. _____ is one of the worst ways to _____.

5. Are you more like Ellen and David or Andy and Pam?

a. Are you more like _____ or _____?

b. Are you more _____ or _____?

Speaking Activities

Dialogue Completion

Complete the following dialogue.

A: What kind of _____ do you like?

B: I like playing basketball and swimming. And you?

A: I like _____, too. Especially during the _____ vacation.

B: How _____ do you go swimming?

A: I don't have much _____, so I just go swimming on _____.
   And you?

B: _____ two days. Do you go swimming alone?

A: Yes, but sometimes I invite my sister to go with me. She thinks it costs a lot.

B: How _____ does it _____?

A: It _____ one hundred and eighty dollars.

B: There is a swimming _____ at school, and it's free.

A: Really? Next time, I will give it a try.

Conversation Practice

A is the coach in a health club. B is a woman who wants to lose weight. They are in the lobby of the club.

A: Welcome to our club. May I help you?

B: Yes, I want to lost weight. What classes should I take?

A: You can take aerobics classes.

B: How much should I pay for the classes and when can I start? You know, I am a housekeeper; I don't have much time and money.

A: Don't worry. We have a promotion now. We give a 20 percent discount and that will be twelve thousand dollars a year. And, you can start tomorrow.

B: OK. It appeals to me. What should I bring with me tomorrow?

A: You should bring your sportswear.

B: Good, see you tomorrow.

A: See you.

Role-play

Find a partner to practice the following dialogue.

Sherry meets her friend, Brian, who is on his way to a health club.

S: Hey, Brian.

B: Hi, Sherry. Long time no see.

S: How come you look so great?

B: Well, I think that's because I make myself committed to workouts at a health club everyday. After work, I spend some time doing vigorous exercise at the club. I particularly enjoy the aerobics classes.

S: I see, and that's why you lose so much weight. In fact, I also want to take off some weight. I am on a diet now.

B: You should do some exercise. You know, exercise is the best way to lose weight and it helps achieve health benefits, too.

S: I know that, but for me the word "exercise" conjures up hours of boring, strenuous activities.

B: It's not like that. Health benefits can be achieved with non-strenuous exercise. You may go for a walk after lunch to boost your metabolism, or use the stairs instead of the elevator to work off calories.

S: That sounds nice. May be I should give it a try. I hope next time when you see me, you won't see my spare tires.

Listening Activities

Listening Comprehension Practice I

Listen to the tape, and answer the questions according to the text you read.

1. (   )   2. (   )   3. (   )   4. (   )   5. (   )

Listening Comprehension Practice II

Listen to the statements on tape, and choose one sport from the word list that is suitable for each of the people in the statements to get.

hiking   gardening   walking   aerobics classes   cycling

1. _____   2. _____   3. _____   4. _____

5. _____

Sentence Dictation

Listen to the sentences on tape, and then fill in the blanks with the missing words.

1. Ellen and David believe in the _____ ,"No pains, no gains."

2. The important thing is to be _____ and make exercise part of your daily life.

3. Use the stairs _____ of the _____ whenever you can.

4. You can be _____ about exercise without _____ it too seriously.

5. There are many ways to _____ this without buying _____ _____ or joining a _____ _____ .

Sentence Memory

Listen to the sentences on tape. If the two sentences you hear mean the same, put "S" in the blank; if not, put "D" in the blank.

1. _____   2. _____   3. _____   4. _____   5. _____

6. _____   7. _____   8. _____   9. _____   10. _____

Listen and Answer

Listen to the narrations and questions on tape. Then answer the questions by completing the following sentences.

1. They spend at least _____ doing exercise every day.

2. Exercise is important because it _____ .

3. No, health benefits can be achieved with _____ .

4. _____ are the ways to stay health without spending too much money.

5. _____ can protect our immune system.

Dialogue Comprehension

Listen to the dialogues on tape. Then answer the questions by completing the following sentences.

1. They spend _____.

2. That's because it can help us keep _____.

3. They are _____.

4. _____ should do at least 30 minutes of moderate activity most days of the week.

5. No, _____.

Writing Activities

Sentence Completion

Use your own words to complete the following sentences.

1. There are many ways to _____.

2. Exercise is important in _____.

3. Every adult should _____.

4. We should spend _____.

5. We all know that _____.

Sentence Scrambling

Re-arrange the given chunks of words to form grammatical sentences.

1. this/expensive equipment/there are many ways/without/to achieve/buying

    → _____

2. you can/without/be serious/exercise/taking it too seriously/about

    → _____

3. that/is important in/healthy/we all know/keeping the body/exercise

    → _____

4. most days of the week/at least/of moderate activity/every adult should/do/30 minutes

→ _____

5. whenever/use the stairs/the elevator/instead of/you can

→ _____

Translation

Translate the following Chinese sentences into English.

1. 沒有不勞而獲的事。

   No _____, no _____.

2. 運動對於保持身體健康及降低疾病風險是重要的。

   Exercise is important in _____ the body healthy and _____ the

   _____ of disease.

3. 他們兩個每天下班後就去，並至少花一小時做劇烈的運動。

   They both go every day _____ _____ and spend at least one

   hour doing _____ exercise.

4. 重要的是要持續並使運動成為你日常生活的一部分。

   The important thing is to be _____ and make exercise part of your

   _____ life.

5. 記住，你可以認真運動但不必把它看得太嚴肅。

   Remember, you can be _____ about exercise without taking it too

   _____.

Error Correction

*In the following passage, some underlined parts are grammatically incorrect and
some are not. Correct the errors, or put a "○" in the blank if the underlined part
is correct.*

> There are many ways to achieve this without (1) <u>buy</u> expensive equipment or (2) <u>join</u> a health club. (3) <u>Walk</u> is one of the best (4) <u>way</u> to get exercise. Try to go for (5) <u>a walk</u> after lunch or dinner (6) <u>for boosting</u> your metabolism and (7) <u>work</u> of some calories. If possible, walk all or (8) <u>part</u> of the way to work or school. As for sports, (9) <u>even that</u> tennis or golf doesn't appeal to you, hiking and cycling can be relaxing and beneficial, too.

Answers:

(1) _____   (2) _____   (3) _____

(4) _____   (5) _____   (6) _____

(7) _____   (8) _____   (9) _____

Free Writing

Name one of your favorite sports. Give three reasons why you particularly like it.

My favorite sport is _____.

First, I like it because _____.

Second, _____.

Finally, _____.

Unit Seven

Fashions

 Pre-reading Activities

Recognize New Words

Learn the Chinese definition of each bold-faced word in the following before you read the text.

1. new **fashions** in the shops   流行式樣
2. colors and **styles**   流行式樣；款式
3. **tight-fitting** clothes   緊身的
4. **fashionable**   流行的；時髦的

5. **baggy** clothes	寬鬆的
6. thirty **centimeters**	公分
7. became **trendy**	時髦的；流行的
8. small **collars**	衣領
9. became **out-dated**	舊式的；過時的
10. look **old-fashioned**	過時的
11. **conservative**	舊式的
12. **traditional**	傳統的
13. seem **stylish**	時髦的；流行的
14. **keep up with** the fashions	跟上…
15. **out of fashion**	不合時尚的
16. **in fashion**	正在流行

Brainstorming Questions

Discuss the following questions with your group members.

1. How can you tell if a man's shirt is trendy?

2. What is the right length for a woman's skirt?

3. What is the best way to keep up with the fashions without spending too much money?

4. How often does a new fashion come out?

Read the Text

Spring, summer, autumn, winter: every season, there are new clothes and new fashions in the shops. Colors and styles keep changing. One season, black is the 'in' color, but the next season everyone is wearing orange or pink or grey. One season,

tight-fitting clothes are fashionable, and the next season baggy   5
clothes are 'in.'

The length of women's skirts goes up and down from year to
year. In the 1960s, mini skirts became very fashionable and a
woman could wear a skirt twenty or thirty centimeters above the
knee. A few years later, maxi skirts became trendy and then you   10
had to wear skirts twenty or thirty centimeters below the knee.
Each season there is always a 'correct' length and if your skirt is
just a little too long or too short some people will think that you
are very unfashionable.

Men have similar problems with their shirts. Some years, it is   15
fashionable to wear very small collars. Another year, small
collars become out-dated and large button-down collars are
trendy. Sometimes it even becomes fashionable to wear shirts
with no collars at all. A shirt that you once thought was very
trendy can look strangely old-fashioned a few years later. And   20
your father's shirts, which you always thought were very
conservative and traditional, can suddenly seem very stylish.

Keeping up with the fashions can be very expensive. So one
way to save money is never to throw your old clothes out. If you
wait long enough, the clothes that are out of fashion today will be   25
back in fashion tomorrow. Yesterday's clothes are tomorrow's
new fashions.

Reading Comprehension Check

*I: According to the text you read, put "T" in the blank if the statement is true; put
"F" if it is not.*

(　　) 1. New fashions come out every season.

(　　) 2. Mini skirts are always in fashion.

(　　) 3. The fashionable length for a woman's skirt depends on the woman's height.

(　　) 4. It's a good idea to keep your parents' old clothes because they are conservative.

(　　) 5. You can tell if a man's shirt is trendy by looking at the collar.

II: According to the text you read, answer the following questions by completing the sentences below.

1. What will people think if your skirt doesn't have a "correct" length?

　→ They will think that I am _____.

2. When were mini skirts quite fashionable?

　→ In _____, they were fashionable.

3. When it comes to clothes, what keeps changing every season?

　→ _____ keep changing.

4. How to keep up with the fashions without spending too much money?

　→ Don't _____.

5. Why not throw your old clothes out?

　→ That's because _____.

III: According to the text you read, choose the best answer to each of the following questions.

(　　) 1. New fashions comes out every _____.

　　　(A) season　(B) year　(C) month　(D) day

(　　) 2. You can tell if a woman's skirt is in fashion by its _____.

　　　(A) color　(B) length　(C) buttons　(D) style

(　) 3. What kind of shirt is fashionable?

　　　(A) Shirts with small collars.

　　　(B) Shirts with button-down collars.

　　　(C) It depends on the trend of the year.

　　　(D) Shirts with no collars.

(　) 4. The best way to keep in fashion without spending too much money is

　　　＿＿＿＿＿.

　　　(A) buying all kinds of clothes at one time

　　　(B) always wearing the old-fashioned clothes

　　　(C) throwing your old clothes away

　　　(D) keeping your old clothes

(　) 5. Baggy clothes are ＿＿＿＿＿.

　　　(A) always in fashion　　(B) sometimes unfashionable

　　　(C) always conservative　(D) seldom popular

(　) 6. What kind of skirt is fashionable in the 1960s?

　　　(A) The skirt that is ten centimeters above the knee.

　　　(B) The skirt that is ten centimeters below the knee.

　　　(C) The skirt that is twenty centimeters above the knee.

　　　(D) The skirt that is thirty centimeters below the knee.

(　) 7. Tight-fitting clothes are ＿＿＿＿＿.

　　　(A) always in fashion　　(B) never in fashion

　　　(C) always conservative　(D) sometimes unfashionable

(　) 8. Traditional shirts can be ＿＿＿＿＿ someday.

　　　(A) out of fashion　(B) stylish　(C) unfashionable　(D) out-dated

Developing Linguistic Ability

Vocabulary Development

Synonyms: Give one proper synonym to each of the following words.

1. fashion → _____   4. fashionable → _____

2. style → _____   5. out-dated → _____

3. baggy → _____   6. traditional → _____

Antonyms: Give one antonym to each of the following words.

1. fashionable → _____   4. tight → _____

2. unfashionable → _____   5. in fashion → _____

3. baggy → _____

Morphology

I: The prefix 'in-,' 'im-' or 'un-' means 'no/not.' Add one of them to each of the following words to form a different word.

1. expensive → _____   4. possible → _____

2. correct → _____   5. patient → _____

3. fashionable → _____   6. happy → _____

II: Add the suffix '-tion' to each of the following words to form the noun.

1. correct → _____   4. indicate → _____

2. observe → _____   5. celebrate → _____

3. conserve → _____   6. connect → _____

Vocabulary Definition

Match each of the words in the left column with its proper definition given in the right column.

_____ 1. baggy   (A) no longer in general use

_____ 2. trendy   (B) design

_____ 3. conservative   (C) loose, not tight

_____ 4. style   (E) rather small and fit closely to the body

_____ 5. out-dated   (F) the part of a shirt that fits round the neck

_____ 6. fashion   (G) the way of dressing that is considered the
                                      best at a certain time

_____ 7. tight-fitting   (H) fashionable

_____ 8. collar   (I) conventional

Vocabulary in Use

Choose the correct answers.

(   ) 1. A few years later, maxi skirts became _____ and then you had
         to wear skirts twenty or thirty centimeters below the knee.
         (A) lengthy   (B) trendy   (C) out-dated   (D) unfashionable

(   ) 2. This season black and grey are the _____ colors, so everybody
         is wearing black or grey.
         (A) on   (B) with   (C) in   (D) above

(   ) 3. My mother is too _____ to wear tight-fitting clothes.
         (A) mild   (B) graceful   (C) attractive   (D) conservative

(   ) 4. The clothes that are out of fashion today may be _____ in fash-
         ion tomorrow.
         (A) returned   (B) back   (C) behind   (D) backwards

(   ) 5. _____ clothes are more comfortable than tight ones.

(A) Baggy　(B) Long　(C) Small　(D) Tiny

(　) 6. Clothes in the 1960s will be ＿＿＿＿＿＿＿ next season.

(A) traditional　(B) stylish　(C) conservative　(D) suitable

(　) 7. The ＿＿＿＿＿＿＿ of women's skirts goes up and down from year to year.

(A) size　(B) width　(C) length　(D) depth

(　) 8. Tina wore a mini skirt twenty or thirty centimeters ＿＿＿＿＿＿＿ the knee.

(A) above　(B) below　(C) beyond　(D) beneath

(　) 9. Her husband likes to wear shirts with large ＿＿＿＿＿＿＿ collars instead of with very small ones.

(A) buttons-up　(B) button-down　(C) button up　(D) buttons down

(　) 10. Every season, there are new fashions in the shops. Colors and styles keep ＿＿＿＿＿＿＿.

(A) changed　(B) changeable　(C) changeless　(D) changing

Phrase in Use

Choose the correct answers.

(　) 1. The length of women's skirts ＿＿＿＿＿＿＿ from year to year.

(A) go up and down　(B) goes up and down

(C) walks back and forth　(D) buttons up

(　) 2. ＿＿＿＿＿＿＿ the fashions can be very expensive.

(A) Staying out　(B) Run after

(C) Go with　(D) Keeping up with

(　) 3. If your skirt is just a little too long or too short, people will think that you're ＿＿＿＿＿＿＿.

(A) out of fashion　(B) in fashion　(C) on time　(D) in time

(   ) 4. Customs differ _____ country _____ country.

     (A) to...from   (B) up...down   (C) from...to   (D) down...up

(   ) 5. Everyone is wearing pink or grey; the two colors are _____ this season.

     (A) in fashion   (B) out of fashion   (C) out of date   (D) out of time

Structure Imitation

Follow the sentence structures given below to create your own sentences.

1. Men have similar problems with their shirts.

    a. _____ similar problems _____ their _____.

    b. _____ the same problems with _____.

2. It becomes fashionable to wear shirts with no collars at all.

    a. It becomes _____ to _____ among youngsters.

    b. It becomes _____ to _____.

3. One way to save money is never to throw your old clothes out.

    a. One way to _____ is never _____.

    b. One way to _____ is _____.

4. If you wait long enough, the old fashion will be back again.

    a. If you wait long enough, you will _____.

    b. If you become _____ enough, _____.

5. Your father's shirts, which you thought were conservative, can suddenly seem very stylish.

    a. Your father's shirts, which _____, may be _____.

    b. Your _____, who _____, may _____.

Structure Focus

Choose the correct answers.

(　　) 1. The length of women's skirts ＿＿＿＿＿＿＿＿＿＿ from year to year.

　　　 (A) are always long　　　　　　(B) like changing

　　　 (C) goes up and down　　　　　(D) became fashionable

(　　) 2. Keeping up with the fashions ＿＿＿＿＿＿＿＿＿＿.

　　　 (A) but takes time　　　　　　 (B) can be very expensive

　　　 (C) always spends time　　　　 (D) really troubling

(　　) 3. Sometimes it became fashionable to wear shirts ＿＿＿＿＿＿＿＿＿.

　　　 (A) with no collars at all　　　 (B) have small collars

　　　 (C) who have big collars　　　 (D) that has no collars

(　　) 4. Your mother's clothes ＿＿＿＿＿＿＿＿＿＿ can be very stylish some-day.

　　　 (A) that were out-dated　　　　(B) who were unfashionable

　　　 (C) should be thrown out　　　 (D) are not your style

(　　) 5. A shirt ＿＿＿＿＿＿＿＿＿＿ can look strangely old-fashioned a few years later.

　　　 (A) are beautiful today　　　　(B) being your father's favorite one

　　　 (C) which in fashion　　　　　(D) you like very much

 *Speaking Activities*

Role Play

Find a partner to practice the following dialogue.

Julia and Catherine are talking about the fashions.

Julia: Hi, Catherine! Have you read the latest *VOGUE* magazine?

Catherine: Not yet. Any new fashions? I am going to buy some pants and skirts.

Julia: Yes, you bet. This year leather pants and grey pants are in fashion. As to skirts, camel skirts and A-line skirts will be fashionable.

Catherine: Oh, no. Last year, I spent lots of money buying mini skirts and black jeans, and they are out of fashion this year.

Julia: You know, fashions keep changing, and you can never catch up with them.

Catherine: You're right. By the way, remember the party on Sunday?

Julia: Sure! I have been thinking about what I should wear to the party these days.

Catherine: Have you got any idea?

Julia: Yah, I probably will wear a V-neck sweater and an A-line skirt. As to shoes, I think I will wear flat boots. Besides, I will bring a cow-print bag with me. And you?

Catherine: I think I will wear a shirt, a mini skirt, and halfboots. My mom will lend me the shirt. I always thought it's old-fashioned, but now it's 'in.'

Julia: That's smart. You know, clothes that are in fashion this season may be out of fashion next season. Keeping up with the fashions can be very expensive. So one way to save money is to keep your parents' old clothes.

Catherine: That's right!

Dialogue Drill

Find a partner to practice the following dialogue.

Judy and Mendy are good friends in college. Mendy is a girl who tries to keep up with the fashions all the time. Now, she is in a department store researching for something " in" with Judy.

Judy: Look at the pink skirt over there. According to the VOGUE magazine, it's the most fashionable color this season.

Mendy: But, its style is out of fashion. It was trendy last season, not now. Besides, mini skirts are stylish this season, and that skirt is long below the knee.

Judy: Ok, forget about it. How about the pink mini skirt? It's exactly what you said.

Mendy: That's it. Now let's try it on, and see if it looks good on us.

(They wear the skirt and look at each other in the mirror.)

Mendy: Wow, you look pretty in it. The fashion this season is just your type. You should buy it. I also want to buy it, although it's not as good on me as on you.

Judy: I like it, too, but it's too expensive.

Mendy: Oh, yes, you're right. We cannot afford it.

Judy: Maybe we can buy it when it's on sale.

Interview Survey

This survey is aimed at understanding how much consumers are aware of fashions. Interview a person and fill out the form.

[Survey Sheet]

1. Sex: _____ (Female/Male)

2. Age: _____

3. Career: _____

4. Marriage: _____ (Single/Married)

5. Where do you usually get information about fashions?

   ☐ TV.   ☐ Magazines/Newspapers.   ☐ Peers/Friends.

   ☐ Others: _____

6. How often do you go to a fashion show?

   ☐ Frequently.   ☐ Sometimes.   ☐ Seldom.   ☐ Never.

7. How much do you usually spend on clothing each season?

   ☐ Less than one-tenth of your salary.

   ☐ About one-fifth of your salary.

   ☐ Over one-second of your salary.

   ☐ Other: _____

8. What do you care more in choosing clothing?

   ☐ Age.   ☐ Fashion.   ☐ Your own style.

   ☐ Others: _____

9. When do you purchase clothes?

   ☐ At the beginning of the season.

   ☐ When clothes are on sale.

   ☐ Only when you need some.

   ☐ Others: _____

10. What does the word "fashions" mean to you?

   ☐ Expensive.   ☐ Beautiful.   ☐ Unique.

   ☐ Others: _____

11. What's the "in" color this season?

12. What's the most fashionable style of clothes this season?

_____

 *Listening Activities*

Sentence Dictation

Listen to the tape and fill in the blanks with the missing words.

1. Spring, summer, autumn, winter: every _____ there are new _____ and new _____ in the shops.

2. The _____ of women's skirts goes _____ and _____ from year to year.

3. Each season there is always a '_____' length and if your skirt is just too _____ or too short some people will think that you are very _____.

4. A shirt that you once thought was very _____ can look strangely _____ a few years later.

5. Keeping up with the fashions can be very _____. So one way to _____ money is never to _____ your old clothes _____.

Sentence Comprehension

If the sentence you hear on tape means the same as the one you read below, put "S" in the blank; if not, put "D" in the blank.

_____ 1. It becomes fashionable to wear a skirt twenty centimeters above the knee.

_____ 2. Keeping up with the fashions can be very expensive.

_____ 3. If you wait long enough, the clothes that are out of fashion today will be back in fashion tomorrow.

_____ 4. Your father's shirts, which you thought were very conservative, can suddenly become very stylish.

_____ 5. One way to save money is never to throw your old clothes out.

Sentence Memory

Listen to the sentences on tape. If the two sentences you hear mean the same, put "S" in the blank; if not, put "D" in the blank.

1. _____   2. _____   3. _____   4. _____   5. _____

Listen and Answer

Listen to the narrations and questions on tape. Then, answer the questions by completing the sentences.

1. _____ keep changing every season.

2. Every season there are _____ in the shops.

3. _____ goes up and down from year to year.

4. _____, mini skirts became very fashionable and a woman could wear a skirt _____ centimeters above the knee.

5. _____ can be very expensive.

Dialogue Comprehension

Listen to the dialogues on tape, and then answer the questions by completing the following sentences.

1.1 She wears _____.

1.2 She wore it _____.

2. _____ were very fashionable when Peter's dad was in college.

3.1 _____ is the "in" color this year.

3.2 Black was the "in" color _____.

 Writing Activities

Error Correction

In the following passage, some underlined parts are grammatically incorrect and some are not. Correct the errors, or put a "○" in the blank if the underlined part is correct.

Men (1) <u>had</u> similar problems with their shirts. Some years it is (2) <u>fashion</u> to wear very small (3) <u>collar</u>. Another year small collars become (4) <u>out-date</u> and large button-down collars are trendy. Sometimes it even becomes fashionable to wear shirts (5) <u>in</u> no collars at all. A shirt that you once (6) <u>think</u> was very trendy can look old-fashioned in a few years.

Answers:

(1) _____ (2) _____ (3) _____

(4) _____ (5) _____ (6) _____

Sentence Completion

Use your own words to complete the following sentences.

1. If you want to save money, you _____.

2. Keeping up with the fashions can _____.

3. The clothes which _____.

4. If your skirt is just too long or _____.

5. One season black is the "in" color but _____.

Sentence Scrambling

Re-arrange the given chunks of words to form grammatical sentences.

1. women's/the/skirts/length/up and down/goes/from year to year/of

   → _____ .

2. their shirts/have/problems/men/similar/with

   → _____ .

3. with the fashions/up/can/very/be/expensive/keeping

   → _____ .

4. fashionable/became/mini/in the 1960s/skirts

   → _____ .

5. tight-fitting clothes/one/fashionable/season/are

   → _____ .

Translation

Translate each of the following Chinese sentences into English.

1. 這衣服現在不流行了。

   This dress is _____ of _____ now.

2. 他穿著時髦。

   He is a s_____ dresser. = He dresses himself s_____ .

3. 我一把抓住他的領子。

   I seized him _____ the _____ .

4. 緊身的衣服現在很流行。

   _____ clothes are very f_____ now.

5. 如今迷你裙不再流行了。

   Today mini skirts have gone _____ of _____ .

6. 每個季節都有新的衣服和流行。

   There are new clothes and _____ every _____ .

123

7. 也許在某一季緊身衣是流行的，到了下一季寬鬆的衣服卻是主流。

Maybe one season _____ clothes are f_____, and the next

season _____ clothes are _____.

8. 在 1960 年代，迷你裙很流行。如果你的裙子太長，有人會認為你落伍了。

In _____ _____, mini skirts were very f_____. If your

skirts were too long, some people would think that you were u_____.

9. 那些你總是認為太保守或者是太傳統的衣服可能會忽然變得很時髦。

The clothes which you always thought were very _____ and

_____ can suddenly become very s_____.

10. 所以，如果你可以等得夠久的話，昨天的衣服明天可能成為新流行。

So, if you wait _____ _____, yesterday's clothes are tomor-

row's new _____.

Unit Eight

Retirement

 Pre-reading Activities

Recognize New Words

Learn the Chinese definition of each bold-faced word in the following before you read the text.

1.	**Protestant immigrants**	清教徒移民
2.	**work ethic**	工作倫理（觀）
3.	**psychological** needs	心理上的
4.	being **productive**	有生產力的

5. their work **defines** them	下定義
6. **retire**	退休 (*v.*)
7. **retirement**	退休 (*n.*)
8. **look forward to** retiring	期盼
9. **financial** problems	財務的
10. **rely on Social Security checks**	依賴社會救濟金支票
11. **contribute** their salaries **to** the government	給予；貢獻
12. **senior citizens**	年長的公民
13. **make ends meet**	使收支平衡
14. the rate of **inflation**	通貨膨脹
15. **Medicare and welfare**	（美國）醫療保險制度與福利
16. can **afford to** buy fuel	負擔得起
17. other **necessities**	必需品
18. **volunteer** work	志願的
19. **respond to** its needs	回應

Brainstorming Questions

Discuss the following questions with your group members.

1. Are your parents already retired? If yes, why did they retire?

2. When would you like to retire?

3. What would you like to do after retiring?

Read the Text

Work is a very important part of life in the United States. When the early Protestant immigrants came to this country, they brought the idea that work was the way to God and heaven. This attitude, the Protestant work ethic, still influences America today. Work is not only important for economic benefits, the salary, but also for social and psychological needs, the feeling of doing something for the good of the society. Americans spend most of their lives working, being productive. For most Americans, their work defines them: They are what they do. What happens, then, when a person can no longer work? 10

Most Americans stop working at age 65 or 70 and retire. Because work is such an important part of life in this culture, retirement can be very difficult. Some retirees feel that they are useless and unproductive. Of course, some people are happy to retire; but leaving one's job, whatever it is, is a difficult change, 15 even for those who look forward to retiring. Many retirees do not know how to use their time, or they feel lost without their jobs.

Retirement can also bring financial problems. Many people rely on Social Security checks every month. During their working years, employees contribute a certain percentage of their 20 salaries to the government. Each employer also gives a certain percentage to the government. When people retire, they receive this money as income. These checks do not provide enough money to live on, however, because prices are increasing very rapidly. Senior citizens, those over age 65, have to have savings 25 in the bank or other retirement plans to make ends meet. The rate of inflation is forcing prices higher each year; Social Security checks alone cannot cover these growing expenses. The government offers some assistance, Medicare (health care) and welfare

(general assistance), but many senior citizens have to change 30
their lifestyles after retirement. They have to spend carefully to
be sure that they can afford to buy food, fuel, and other necessities.

Of course, many senior citizens are happy with retirement.
They have time to spend with their families or to enjoy their 35
hobbies. Some continue to work part-time; others do volunteer
work. Some, like those in the Retired Business Executives
Association, even help young people to get started in new
businesses. Many retired citizens also belong to "Golden Age"
groups. These organizations plan trips and social events. There 40
are many opportunities for retirees.

American society is only beginning to be concerned about
the special physical and emotional needs of its senior citizens.
The government is taking steps to ease the problem of limited
income. It is building new housing, offering discounts in stores 45
and museums and on buses, and providing other services, such
as free classes, food service, and help with housework. Retired
citizens are a rapidly growing percentage of the population. This
part of the population is very important, and we must respond to
its needs. After all, every citizen will be a senior citizen someday. 50

Reading Comprehension Check

I: According to what you read, if the statement is true, put "T" in the blank; if not, put "F" in the blank.

(　　) 1. Work plays an important part of life in America.

(　　) 2. People work simply for economic benefits, the salary, but not for social and psychological needs.

(   ) 3. Americans spend most of their lives working, and keeping productive.

(   ) 4. Most Americans stop working at age 65 or 70 and retire.

(   ) 5. Leaving one's job, anyway, is a difficult change, even for those who hope to retire.

(   ) 6. Many retirees do not know how to use their time, or feel lost without their jobs.

(   ) 7. Most Americans want to be productive, so retirement can be very difficult for them.

(   ) 8. Retirement brings financial problems because most of the retirees have no income at all.

(   ) 9. Not only the Social Security but also the government offers some assistance to the retirees.

(   ) 10. "Golden Age" groups are organizations which provide many opportunities for retirees.

II: According to the text you read, correct the errors in the following statements.
Underline your corrections in the blanks.

1. Retirement also brings social problems to senior citizens.

   _____

2. During their working years, American employees contribute fifty percentage of their salaries to the government.

   _____

3. Those who are over age fifty-five must have savings or other retirement plans to make ends meet.

   _____

4. The government offers sufficient assistance, so many senior citizens don't

have to change their lifestyles after retirement.

_____

5. "Golden Age" groups plan trips and social events for the young people.

_____

III: According to the text you read, answer the following questions by completing sentences below.

1. How do some retirees feel?

   They feel that they are _____.

2. What do many people rely on after they retire?

   They rely on _____ every month.

3. What kind of assistance the government offer to retirees?

   The government offers some assistance to them such as _____

   _____.

4. What do the senior citizens have to do to make ends meet?

   They have to _____ to make ends

   meet.

5. What do people in the Retired Business Executives Association do?

   They help young people _____.

6. What kind of role does work play in American life?

   Work plays _____.

7. How do Americans think of retirement?

   Some retirees feel _____; some are _____.

8. How does the system, the Social Security, work?

   During their working years, employees _____

   _____. Each employer also _____.

   When people retire, _____.

9. Why is the money from the Social Security checks not enough for the retirees to live on?

It's difficult to live by this money because _____

_____. The rate of inflation forces _____

_____.

10. Why are retired citizens important in the society and why should we respond to their needs?

After all, _____.

VI: According to the text you read, choose the best answer to each of the following questions.

(   ) 1. What's a very important part of life in the United States?

(A) Playing.   (B) Work.   (C) Traveling.   (D) Drinking.

(   ) 2. At what age do most Americans retire?

(A) 50 or 55.   (B) 55 or 60.   (C) 60 or 65.   (D) 65 or 70.

(   ) 3. What can many senior citizens do after they retire?

(A) Spend time with their families.   (B) Enjoy their hobbies.

(C) Do volunteer work.   (D) All of the above.

(   ) 4. What do retirees in "Golden Age" groups do?

(A) Plan trips and social events.

(B) Help young people.

(C) Work part-time to afford themselves.

(D) Offer opportunities for young people.

(   ) 5. How do those retirees who don't know how to use their time feel without jobs?

(A) Useful.   (B) Lost.   (C) Satisfied.   (D) Happy.

Cloze Test

Choose the best answer to fill in each blank to make the whole passage meaningful and grammatical.

Retirement can also ____1____ financial problems. Many people ____2____ Social Security checks every month. During their ____3____ years, employees contribute a certain percentage of their salaries ____4____ the government. And each employer does that, ____5____. When people retire, they receive this money ____6____ income. It's difficult to live by this money only, because prices are increasing very ____7____. Those who are over age 65 must have savings or other retirement plans to make ends ____8____. Inflation forces prices ____9____ each year; Social Security alone cannot cover these growing expenses. The government offers some assistance, but many senior citizens have to change their lifestyles after retirement. To ____10____ daily expenses, they must be careful in ____11____.

( ) 1. (A) take   (B) bring   (C) carry   (D) result

( ) 2. (A) rely on   (B) focus on   (C) rely in   (D) depend in

( ) 3. (A) work   (B) working   (C) career   (D) professional

( ) 4. (A) to   (B) for   (C) against   (D) in

( ) 5. (A) however   (B) in the end   (C) either   (D) too

( ) 6. (A) to   (B) as   (C) for   (D) in

( ) 7. (A) rapidly   (B) speedy   (C) gradually   (D) smoothly

( ) 8. (A) to meet   (B) meeting   (C) meet   (D) met

( ) 9. (A) higher   (B) lower   (C) taller   (D) shorter

( ) 10. (A) purchase   (B) resist   (C) buy   (D) afford

( ) 11. (A) spend   (B) spent   (C) earning   (D) spending

Most Americans stop working ____12____ age 65 or 70 and retire. Because work is ____13____ an important part of life in this culture, ____14____ can be very difficult. Some retirees feel that they are ____15____ and unproductive. Of course, some people are happy to retire. Leaving one's job, ____16____, is a difficult change, even for ____17____ hope to retire. Many retirees do not know ____18____ to use their time, ____19____ feel ____20____ without their jobs.

( ) 12. (A) at   (B) in   (C) during   (D) while

( ) 13. (A) so   (B) such   (C) even   (D) much

( ) 14. (A) retirement   (B) employment   (C) enrichment   (D) agreement

( ) 15. (A) useful   (B) useless   (C) helpful   (D) valuable

( ) 16. (A) therefore   (B) accordingly   (C) anyway   (D) thus

( ) 17. (A) whom   (B) the one that   (C) who   (D) those who

( ) 18. (A) how   (B) what   (C) when   (D) where

( ) 19. (A) or   (B) because   (C) however   (D) but

( ) 20. (A) losing   (B) loss   (C) lost   (D) loose

Developing Linguistic Ability

Vocabulary Development

Synonyms: Give one synonym to each of the following words.

1. influence (*v.*) → _____

2. rely → _____

3. assistance → _____

4. opportunity → _____

5. rapidly → _____

6. benefit → _____

Antonyms: Give one antonym to each of the following words.

1. useless → _____

2. immigrant → _____

4. productive → _____

5. psychological → _____

3. employee → _____   6. increasing → _____

Morphology

I: Form a different word by adding the prefix 'in-,' 'im-' or 'un-' which means 'no/not' to the beginning of each following word.

1. expensive → _____   4. proper → _____

2. necessary → _____   5. important → _____

3. productive → _____   6. cover → _____

II: Form a noun by adding a suffix such as '-tion' to the end of each following word.

1. happy → _____   4. grow → _____

2. retire → _____   5. provide → _____

3. productive → _____   6. close → _____

Word Definition

Match each of the words in the left column with its proper definition given in the right column.

_____ 1. inflation   (A) connected with money

_____ 2. productive   (B) something that needs to have

_____ 3. retirement   (C) well-being; comfort and good health

_____ 4. define   (D) to join with others in giving (money or help)

_____ 5. immigrant   (E) the condition in which prices keep rising

_____ 6. financial   (F) to give the meaning of something

_____ 7. psychological   (G) a person who come into a country to make his or

_____ 8. contribute   her life and home there

_____ 9. welfare   (H) the period after one has stopped working

_____10. necessity   (I) connected with the way that the mind works

(J) very efficient at what one does

Vocabulary in Use

Choose the correct answers.

(　)　1. He was a _____ writer; he wrote lots of books.

(A) financial　(B) sad　(C) productive　(D) happy

(　)　2. Tom's loss of memory is a _____ problem, rather than a physical one.

(A) healthy　(B) psychological　(C) biological　(D) geographic

(　)　3. Some words are hard to _____. It's hard to give them exact meanings.

(A) define　(B) find　(C) read　(D) write

(　)　4. Illness forced him to _____ from office.

(A) retire　(B) work　(C) come　(D) get

(　)　5. Peter lost lots of money; now he has _____ problems.

(A) healthy　(B) financial　(C) physical　(D) mental

(　)　6. Mother Teresa devoted her life to the _____ of the poor.

(A) illness　(B) retirement　(C) welfare　(D) inflation

(　)　7. The car is too expensive; I cannot _____ it.

(A) afford　(B) define　(C) drive　(D) retire

(　)　8. This work costs us nothing; it's all done by _____.

(A) employees　(B) employer　(C) workers　(D) volunteers

(　)　9. The police did not _____ to the terrorists' demands.

(A) respond　(B) ask　(C) receive　(D) accept

(　) 10. Food is a _____ of life.

(A) walfare　(B) part　(C) necessity　(D) portion

Phrase in Use

Choose the correct answers.

(　　) 1. Many people ＿＿＿＿＿＿ Social Security checks every month after
retirement.

(A) go on　(B) keep on　(C) rely on　(D) put on

(　　) 2. Work is ＿＿＿＿＿＿ important for economic benefits ＿＿＿＿＿＿
for social and psychological needs.

(A) either...or　(B) not only...but also

(C) neither...nor　(D) whether...or not

(　　) 3. I'm ＿＿＿＿＿＿ meeting you.

(A) looking at　(B) looking around

(C) looking up to　(D) looking forward to

(　　) 4. It's difficult to ＿＿＿＿＿＿ on her husband's small salary.

(A) make ends meet　(B) make it up　(C) make up for　(D) make up to

(　　) 5. Many retired citizens also ＿＿＿＿＿＿ "Golden Age" groups.

(A) link with　(B) connect to　(C) have to　(D) belong to

Structure Focus

Follow the sentence structures given below to create your own sentences.

1. For most Americans, work is such an important part of life.

　a. For ＿＿＿＿＿＿＿＿＿＿＿＿, work ＿＿＿＿＿＿＿＿＿＿＿＿.

　b. For a retired person, ＿＿＿＿＿＿＿＿＿＿＿＿＿＿＿＿.

2. Some people feel that they are useless and unproductive when they retire.

　a. Some ＿＿＿＿＿＿＿＿＿＿＿, when ＿＿＿＿＿＿＿＿＿＿＿.

　b. Some retirees do not know ＿＿＿＿＿＿＿＿＿＿＿, or ＿＿＿＿＿＿＿
＿＿＿＿＿＿ without their jobs.

3. Work is not only important for economic benefits, the salary, but also for social
and psychological needs.

　a. ＿＿＿＿＿＿＿＿＿＿＿ is both important for ＿＿＿＿＿＿＿＿＿＿＿

and for _____.

b. It's _____ for retired people to _____

every month, because _____.

4. Some continue to work part-time; others do volunteer work.

a. Some _____; others _____.

b. Some decide to _____; others _____.

5. When the early Protestant immigrants came to this country, they brought the

idea that work was the way to God and heaven.

a. When _____ came to _____,

they _____.

b. When I _____, I _____.

Speaking Activities

Dialogue Completion

Complete the following dialogue.

(A husband and his wife are talking about their retirement plan.)

H: Now we have a lot of time doing our favorite activities together.

W: Yes, but let's make a retirement _____. I've heard some people were lost

and felt _____ and _____ after retirement.

H: Don't worry. I do have a plan. First, we can go _____ to Europe, like

France and Italy.

W: That _____ wonderful! But before that we visit our grandchildren and

old friends in other cities.

H: Of course. As a _____ of fact, I've planned that we will visit some of our

grandchildren in Kaohsiung City. Can you imagine how tall _____ now?

I can't wait to see them.

W: Me, too. I am glad you _____ made the plan.

H: By the way, Lily, our granddaughter in Tai-Dong is sick. Should we go and see her first, or shall we _____ my plan?

W: What happened? _____ is she now?

H: Not too bad. If we go to see her first, then, we have to give up my plan and make a new one.

W: Well, we had better postpone our plan of traveling to Europe.

H: Okay. That's fine. After all, we still have plenty of _____, right?

Interview

Interview a person. You play the role of A and fill out the form.

[Interview Sheet]

A: At what age do you retire from your work?

B: _____

A: How do you feel after retirement?

B: _____

A: What do you do most of the time every day?

B: _____

_____

A: Do you sometimes feel useless? Give the reasons.

B: _____

_____

A: Do you get any financial support from the government?

B: _____

A: Do you get any money from your children?

B: _____

A: What is the best retirement plan in your opinion?

B: _____

_____

Listening Activities

Sentence Comprehension

If the sentence you hear on tape means the same as the one you read below, put "S" in the blank; if not, put "D" in the blank.

_____ 1. Work is a very important part of life in the United States.

_____ 2. This attitude, the Protestant work ethic, still influences Americans today.

_____ 3. Because work is such an important part of life in this culture, retirement can be very difficult.

_____ 4. "Golden Age" groups plan trips and social events.

_____ 5. Social Security checks do not provide enough money to live on, however, because prices are increasing very rapidly.

Sentence Dictation

Listen to the tape, and then fill in the blanks with the missing words.

1. When the early Protestant _____ came to this country, they brought the _____ that work was the way to God and heaven.

2. Work is not only important for _____ benefits, but also for social and _____ needs.

3. Because work is such an important part of life in American _____, retirement can be very _____.

4. Many _____ do not know how to use their time, or they feel

_____ without their jobs.

5. The government offers some _____, but many senior citizens have to change their _____ after retirement.

Sentence Memory

Listen to the sentences on tape. If the two sentences you hear mean the same, put "S" in the blank; if not, put "D" in the blank.

1. _____   2. _____   3. _____   4. _____   5. _____

Listen and Answer

Listen to the narrations and questions on tape. Then, answer the questions by completing the following sentences.

1. _____ brought the idea to America that work was the way to God and heaven.

2. They feel they are useless and unproductive because _____

_____.

3. They rely on _____ every month.

4. They must have _____ or other _____.

5. Because many retirees do not know _____ or feel _____ without their jobs.

Writing Activities

Sentence Scrambling

Re-arrange the given chunks of words to form grammatical sentences.

1. not only/is/work/for economic benefits/but also/important/for social and

psychological needs

→ _____

2. look forward to/a difficult change/is/retiring/leaving one's job/even for/those who

→ _____

3. they/to enjoy/to spend/have time/with their families/their hobbies/or

→ _____

4. continue/part-time/others/do volunteer work/some/to work

→ _____

5. an important part of life/is/such/because/in this culture/can be/very difficult/retirement/work

→ _____

Translation

Translate each of the following Chinese sentences into English.

1. 在美國，工作是生活中重要的一部分。

Work is a very important _____ _____ _____ in the United States.

2. 有些退休的人覺得他們是無用而且無生產力的。

Some _____ feel that they are _____ and _____.

3. 退休也可能帶來財政問題。

_____ can also bring _____ problems.

4. 他們有時間可以和家人團聚或浸淫在他們的嗜好中。

They have time to spend _____ their families or to enjoy their _____.

5. 很多年長的公民在退休之後必須改變他們的生活方式。

Many senior _____ have to change their lifestyles after _____.

Error Correction

In the following passage, some underlined parts are grammatically incorrect and some are not. Correct the errors, or put a "○" in the blank if the underlined part is correct.

Most Americans stop (1) to work at age 65 or 70 and retire. Because work is (2) such an important part of life in this culture, retirement can be difficult. Some retirees feel that they are useless and unproductive. Of course, some people are (3) happily to retire; but (4) leave one's job, (5) whichever it is, is a difficult change, even for those (6) whom look forward to (7) retire. Many retirees do not know (8) how to use their time, (9) or they feel (10) losing without their jobs.

Answers:

(1) _____   (2) _____   (3) _____

(4) _____   (5) _____   (6) _____

(7) _____   (8) _____   (9) _____

(10) _____

Acknowledgments

Stop the Spread of Deserts

From *In Context, Second Edition* by Jean Zukowski/Faust, Susan S. Johnston, and Elizabeth Templin. Copyright © 1996 by Harcourt Brace & Company, reprinted by permission of the publisher.

Welcome to the Web

From *The World Wide Web* by Christopher Lampton, published by Franklin Watts, a division of Grolier Publishing. Copyright © 1997. Reprinted by permission of the publisher.

Communication through Satellite

From *In Context, Second Edition* by Jean Zukowski/Faust, Susan S. Johnston, and Elizabeth Templin. Copyright © 1996 by Harcourt Brace & Company, reprinted by permission of the publisher.

Culture Shock

From *Contact USA, 3ʳᵈ ed.* by Paul Abraham & Daphne Mackey. Copyright © 1997. Reprinted by permission of the publisher.

Procrastination

From *Lado English Series 5* by Lado. Copyright © 1990. Reprinted by permission of Prentice-Hall, Inc., Upper Saddle River, NJ.

Healthwatch: How Much Exercise Do We Really Need?

From *Spectrum 3* by Byrd. Copyright © 1994. Reprinted by permission of Prentice-Hall, Inc., Upper Saddle River, NJ.

一本最符合英語學習者需求的辭典！

三民 全球英漢辭典

莊信正、楊榮華主編

◎ 詞彙蒐羅詳盡，全書詞目超過93,000項。
◎ 釋義清晰明瞭，以樹枝狀的概念，將每個字彙分成「基本義」與「衍生義」，使讀者對字彙的理解更具整體概念。
◎ 以學習者的需要為出發點，將臺灣英語學習者最需要的語言資料詳實涵括在本書各項單元中。
◎ 新增「搭配用詞」一欄，列出詞語間的常用組合，增進你的語感，幫助你寫出、說出道地的英文。

讓你掌握英語的慣用搭配方式，學會道道地地的英語！

三民 新英漢辭典（增訂完美版）

◎ 收錄詞目增至67,500項（詞條增至46,000項）。
◎ 新增「搭配」欄，列出常用詞語間的組合關係，讓你掌握英語的慣用搭配，說出道地的英語。
◎ 附有精美插圖千餘幅，輔助詞義理解。
◎ 附錄包括詳盡的「英文文法總整理」、「發音要領解說」，提升學習效率。

一般辭典查不到的文化意涵，讓它來告訴你！

美國日常語辭典

莊信正、楊榮華主編

◎ 描寫美國真實面貌，讓你不只學好美語，更進一步瞭解美國社會與文化！
◎ 廣泛蒐集美國人日常生活的語彙，是一本能伴你暢遊美國的最佳工具書！
◎ 從日常生活的角度出發，自日常用品、飲食文化、文學、藝術、到常見俚語，帶領你感受美語及其所代表的文化內涵，讓學習美語的過程不再只是背誦單字和強記文法句型的單調練習。

UP-TO-DATE／清楚・明瞭・方便・易查

三民 簡明英漢辭典（全新修訂版）

◎ 內容涵蓋70,074個詞條，從日常生活用語到專業用語，一應俱全。
◎ 大量收錄了符合現代潮流的新辭彙、新語義。
◎ 精準明確的譯義，有助讀者快速理解。
◎ 全書採用K.K.音標，並清楚標示美音／英音差異。
◎ 有＊、※記號的重要字彙，均有套色印刷設計，方便易查。
◎ 輕巧體貼的口袋型設計，便於外出攜帶。

你將會發現：學英語竟然可以這麼自自然然、輕輕鬆鬆！

自然英語會話

大西泰斗著／Paul C. McVay著

用生動、簡單易懂的筆調，針對口語的特殊動詞、日常生活的口頭禪等加強解說，引領你體驗英語精髓，使你的英語會話更接近以英語為母語的人，更加流利、自然。

英文自然學習法（一）

大西泰斗著／Paul C. McVay著

針對被動語態、時態、進行式與完成式、Wh-疑問句與關係詞等重點分析解說，讓你輕鬆掌握英文文法的竅門。

英文自然學習法（二）

大西泰斗著／Paul C. McVay著

打破死背介系詞意義和片語的方式，將介系詞的各種衍生用法連繫起來，讓你自然掌握介系詞的感覺和精神。

英文自然學習法（三）

大西泰斗著／Paul C. McVay著

運用「兔子和鴨子」的原理，解說PRESSURE、MUST、POWER、WILL、UP / DOWN / OUT / OFF等用法的基本觀念，以及所衍生出各式各樣精采豐富的意思，讓你簡單輕鬆活用英語！

第一本專為華人青少年編寫、
以華人生活為主題的英文課外讀物！

黛安的日記 ①

黃啟哲 著／呂亨英 譯

　　如果你認為上英文課已經很苦了，想想看，要是你突然發現要搬到美國，並且必須跟美國小孩一起上學的話，會是什麼情況呢？這事就發生在黛安身上。想知道一個完全不會英文的中國小女孩在美國是怎麼生存的嗎？看黛安的日記吧！

同步口譯教你聽英語

齋藤なが子 著／劉明綱 譯

　　溝通就像打乒乓球一樣，必須見招拆招，並不是每個老外在聽完你的"How are you?"之後，都會回答"Fine, thank you, and you?" 語言是活的，沒有人能以不變應萬變，本書作者以其多年來在第一線同步口譯的親身經歷，告訴你什麼是「聽英語」的訣竅！

老外會怎麼說？

各務行雅 著／鄭維欣 譯

學了這麼多年的英文，
一開口卻還是讓老外一臉疑惑？
作者以留美多年的經驗，
從文化及觀念上的差異，
告訴你真正實用的生活美語！

英 文 文 法

蘇玉如／應惠蕙　編著

全書由基本概念侃侃而談，再按句子的結構
依次介紹各項詞類，並以簡易清晰的範例，
加上生動活潑的單元練習，幫助學生迅速理
解，建立紮實的英文基礎，是輕鬆學習文法
的必備工具。

英 文 文 法 應 用 解 析

蘇玉如／應惠蕙　編著

本書延續《英文文法》的重要文法概念，依
據各章的主題，呈現更豐富的選文與更多樣
化的評量習題。使用這本優良的工具書，學
生必能在歸納與印證的學習歷程中，徹底理
解文法觀念，達到信手拈來皆是精確英文的
境界。

英 文 聽 力 測 驗

Ange Sabine Peter／應惠蕙　著

全書共六冊，分為學生用書、教師用書以及
CD，每冊皆由十二個主題獨立的單元所組
成，內容與日常生活緊密相關，由簡入深，
循序漸進。特聘外籍專業錄音員錄製CD，命
題方向及朗讀速度皆配合全民英語檢定，非
常適合在課堂測驗及課後自修時使用。